GONE ASTRAY

It's every policeman's worst nightmare: a little girl has been abducted, and Falbrough CID can find no trace of her. The department's newest detective, Constable 'Thorny' Deepbriar, one-time village bobby, already has his hands full. He's looking into a spate of robberies, he has two weeks to vacate Minecliff's police house, and his wife Mary, is expecting their first child – years after giving up hope of having a family. However, when Deepbriar discovers a possible connection between the disappearance of Janey Smithers and an incident that his colleagues have swept under the carpet, he can't resist investigating.

GONE ASTRAY

GONE ASTRAY

by

Jean Rowden

Magna Large Print Books
Long Preston, North Yorkshire,
BD23 4ND, England.

British Library Cataloguing in Publication Data.

Rowden, Jean
    Gone astray.

    A catalogue record of this book is
    available from the British Library

    ISBN   978-0-7505-3729-2

First published in Great Britain in 2012 by Robert Hale Ltd.

Copyright © Jean Rowden 2012

Cover illustration by arrangement with Robert Hale Ltd.

Published in Large Print 2013 by arrangement with
Robert Hale Ltd.

Magna Large Print is an imprint of Library Magna Books Ltd.

Printed and bound in Great Britain by
T.J. (International) Ltd., Cornwall, PL28 8RW

*This book is dedicated to Marjorie,
born 16th June, 1912. She is an inspiration,
a lady with a strong will and an indomitable
spirit. What's more, she thinks
my books are 'not bad'.*

Chapter One

Detective Constable Thomas Deepbriar, known to his friends as Thorny, stepped through the front door of Falbrough police station. Leaving behind him the chilly calm of a misty November morning, he entered a scene of total chaos.

An ill-assorted pack of men were milling about in the front office, some of them in business suits and ties, others in overalls; amongst this unlikely mix, and looking even more out of place, were a handful of farm workers, who had apparently come straight from fields or cowsheds. One, a grey-haired ancient, was dressed in a smock, which added to Deepbriar's sense of unreality; he'd not seen anybody dressed in that fashion since his early childhood.

Deepbriar had been looking forward to his first day on duty as a CID officer for many months. It was unsettling to feel that he was adrift, as if he'd walked out of his own life and into the shoes of a stranger. He felt a sudden nostalgia for his years as a village bobby. It was impossible to make his way to the counter, so he sidled round the outside of the room.

9

'Deepbriar, there you are.' His boss, newly promoted Chief Inspector Stubbs, flung open the door of the CID office, and stood beckoning him in, his face set into an uncharacteristically grim expression. 'Jakes says you can't drive. Is that true?'

'Yes sir, I'm sorry,' Deepbriar replied, his bafflement deepening.

'Damn.' Stubbs sighed, evidently caught between resignation and annoyance. Behind him, Sergeant Jakes, tall and gangling, was rising from his desk, his expression expectant, though equally serious. 'All right, Sergeant, it'll have to be you. You'll need to have some driving lessons, Deepbriar, as soon as you can. Meantime, you're holding the fort here until Sergeant Gough gets in; he's being called back from leave, so that might not be until midday. Ask Hubbard for help if you need it.' With a nod he was gone, leaving the door open for Jakes, who was disentangling a scarf from the hat stand.

'What's going on? What's the panic?' Deepbriar appealed as the sergeant went by.

'Honestly, Thorny, don't you country bumpkins listen to the wireless? A little girl's gone missing in Cawster.' Jakes turned to the desk and picked up a file. He tossed it to Deepbriar. 'All we've got is in there, and it's precious little. You'll find the rest of our on-going cases in the top drawer of the filing cabinet; you'd better have a quick scan

10

through those as well. At least that way you'll have an inkling about what's going on if anyone calls.'

A child. As the door closed behind Jakes, Deepbriar sank into a chair. That explained everything; there must have been an appeal for volunteers to join the search. He opened the file. There was no photograph yet; the case must be too recent for one to have reached them. Deepbriar shifted his shoulders uncomfortably; Jakes's jibe had struck home. He didn't listen to the news on the Home Service any more. Mary's first baby was due soon; she was keeping well, but recently she had started crying at anything remotely sad. Unable to cope with a wife so unlike her usual cheerful self, Thorny had unplugged the wireless; for the last two weeks they had eaten their breakfast in silence.

There were only half a dozen pieces of paper in the file. The little girl wasn't merely missing. A man had taken her from a playground on the edge of Cawster, shortly after four o'clock the previous afternoon. The abduction had been seen, at a distance, by a neighbour who was pushing her pram around the other side of the park. Knowing the child, and not recognizing the car, she had been suspicious enough to raise the alarm at once. After flagging down a local builder, who was driving by in his van, she had asked him to try to follow the car while

11

she hurried to the nearest police call-box.

The builder had done his best, but he had lost sight of the car once it turned on to the main road towards Falbrough, where it had driven off at great speed. He was able to tell them only that the car was large, not of a very modern design, and black, which gave the police practically nothing to work on.

Alerted so quickly, the Cawster force had instructed all their officers to watch for the car, but the description was too general, and they had chased dozens of vehicles without getting anywhere. Only one lead appeared promising; a farmer's wife had reported seeing a big saloon car bumping up a lonely track on to the moors. This was at 7.15, long after dark. Two officers had been sent to investigate and a roadblock was set up. Since the vehicle hadn't been seen returning, and the network of unmade roads led only to dead ends, they should have their man trapped. The superintendent had made the appeal for volunteers, in order to start a widespread search at daybreak. Deepbriar had arrived while the final batch were causing mayhem in the outer office, awaiting transport.

As Deepbriar closed the file Sergeant Hubbard came barrelling through the door.

'Being circulated,' he said. He dropped an oblong card on the desk in front of Deepbriar and beat an instant retreat. Thorny pulled a face; he had put Hubbard's nose out of joint when he made the move to CID, but he wasn't going to let it worry him. There were just two words on the card, in Hubbard's crabbed writing. *Janey Smithers.* Turning the card over, Deepbriar felt his heart plunge; the photograph showed a fair-haired girl, her pigtails adorned with bows, and her wide smile accentuating the gaps where two of her front teeth were missing. After studying the face for a moment to be sure he would recognize it, Deepbriar thrust the picture into the cardboard folder, stood up and went to the filing cabinet. He would try to catch up on the department's other current concerns. He sighed as he pulled out the first file; this was turning into one of the days when he wished he had followed his dad's advice and gone to work for the railway.

Once the last of the volunteers had been ferried away the station sank into a state of relative calm. A mood of watchful expectancy hung over the few officers who remained; there was no idle chatter, and when speech was necessary voices were muted.

Gloom descended on Deepbriar as he tried to digest all the details of the CID's recent cases. They were grouped under headings such as actual bodily harm, adultery, and arson; at any other time the fact that bigamy and buggery shared a file, empty at present, might have been mildly amusing, but he moved swiftly on to burglary. Within half an hour Deepbriar had learnt that within the last month Falbrough CID had been investigating a spate of robberies from industrial premises. There had also been an attack on a young woman walking home late at night, several minor thefts and two reports of stolen cars, only one of which looked like a genuine crime. The second had resulted from the owner's over-indulgence at a party, which caused him to forget where he had parked his vehicle for three whole days. The file had been left open, as Sergeant Gough wanted to prosecute the man for wasting police time. Finally there had been a break-in at a country house which had caused a furore because a cabinet minister had been staying there for the weekend; he and his hosts had made their displeasure widely known. Chief Inspector Stubbs was tackling this case himself, in an attempt to keep the owners of the mansion and their illustrious guest happy.

Sergeant Gough still hadn't appeared at midday, and Deepbriar remained in solitary command of the office. When his stomach started to rumble he dashed out to fetch his sandwiches, which he'd left in his bicycle saddlebag. On his return he was waylaid by Sergeant Hubbard.

'There you are. I thought you'd gone AWOL. We've had a report of another factory being broken into. This time they've had a go at Robertson's, the paintworks on Mill Road. Constable Reed just called it in. He's there now, but I want him back on the beat, asap. It's CID's pigeon,' he added, scowling, as if Thorny had argued the point, 'which, since Gough still hasn't turned up, means you, Deepbriar, gawd help us all.'

'How come it's only just been reported? All the other jobs were done at night.'

'How should I know? Working out the whys and wherefores are beyond us simple coppers, that's what they employ brainy people like you for.' Hubbard thrust a slip of paper into Deepbriar's hand and turned away, exchanging a knowing look with the constable who stood behind the enquiry desk. The youngster smirked.

'We'll do our best to keep things running smoothly without you,' the sergeant said, as Deepbriar turned to leave.

Having managed to swallow one sandwich between the back door and his bike, Thorny put the rest of his lunch away again and headed for Mill Road; luckily it wasn't far. Perhaps he really did need to learn to drive if he was ever to be taken seriously as a detective. His two fictional heroes, Dick Bland and the American private eye, Mitch O'Hara, were both demons behind the

15

wheel. At least he was only investigating a minor robbery. Chief Inspector Stubbs was right; now that he was a detective he would feel a fool arriving at a serious crime scene by bicycle. The world was changing, and he had to change with it.

Robertson's premises were scattered over a large area, the whole site being surrounded by a high brick wall. As Deepbriar arrived the lunch whistle sounded, and he pedalled in through the gates against a tide of workers who were heading home for their midday meal. He found Constable Reed in the office with the manager, a florid-faced man called Pearce.

'We hadn't realized we'd been robbed, because nobody came in here this morning,' Pearce said, in answer to Deepbriar's first query. The man rubbed at his already shiny cheeks with a handkerchief as he showed the way into the accounts office. 'Sidebottom, our accounts manager, is off sick. If I'd known that when I came in, I wouldn't have given Walton permission to go on this search you people are doing on the moor. The office shouldn't really be left empty.'

'Walton?' Deepbriar queried.

'The clerk. It was a nasty shock when the constable here came and told me he'd spotted something odd about the window.'

'I was on my beat,' Reed explained. 'When you're coming down Lott's Hill you can see over the top of the wall.'

At first glance the room didn't look much like a crime scene; desks, one large and one small, filled two of the corners, while the opposite wall held a row of filing cabinets and an old-fashioned safe. This appeared to be untouched. The small window that Reed pointed out was above head height. At first Deepbriar could see nothing wrong with it, but when he stood right underneath he realized that only the outer frame remained in place. He stared at the floor; there wasn't a single shard of glass to be seen.

'Have you cleared this up?'

'This is how we found it,' Pearce replied.

'I had a look outside,' Constable Reed put in. 'I don't know how they did it, but the whole window is still in one piece, propped against the wall. They didn't even break the glass.'

'So, what's missing?' Deepbriar circled the desks; the drawers were closed, the few papers left lying about were still in orderly heaps.

Pearce pointed to the top drawer in the larger desk. 'That's normally kept locked, because the petty-cash-box is in there. It held about five pounds, quite a bit more than usual.'

Deepbriar stooped, studying the splinters of wood; it had taken the thief only a second to break the lock. 'You've already looked in here, I take it?' he asked, easing the drawer open without touching the handle; the precaution was almost certainly useless, for no fingerprints had been found after any of the previous robberies.

'Yes, the cash-box has gone. There was a little package in there too, a brooch I'd bought for my wife's birthday on Thursday.' Pearce pulled a rueful face. 'I didn't want anybody finding it before the big day and I thought it would be safer here, with three children at home. Since they and my wife sometimes come into my office, that wasn't ideal either, so I decided to entrust it to Sidebottom.'

'Why didn't you use the safe, sir?' Constable Reed asked disapprovingly.

'It hardly seemed worth fiddling about with a combination. I mean, why would anybody break in for the sake of a few bob in petty cash?' Pearce said. 'We use the safe for the wages of course, on a Friday night. We pay our people at midday Saturday.'

'You'd think the villain would have waited and had a go at something worth while,' Reed commented. 'There's plenty of safe-crackers who wouldn't find that model too difficult to open.'

'It's a bit odd,' Deepbriar agreed. The crime followed the pattern of the previous break-ins; the thief had come and gone without leaving much to work on, but hav-

18

ing climbed the wall, taken out the window and broken into the desk, he'd got away with very little. It seemed like a lot of effort for a few pounds.

'I'll need a description of the brooch,' Deepbriar said.

'I can do better than that,' Pearce replied, 'I got it from Tyler's, in the High Street, and they had another one for sale, exactly the same, apart from the stones. I chose the one with three sapphires; the other's set with emeralds.'

'Right.' Deepbriar glanced at Reed. 'Perhaps you'd pop in there on your way back to the station?' he said hopefully. 'You might ask that the remaining brooch is kept until we've had a chance to photograph it.'

Constable Reed nodded. 'I'll do that, if you'll square it with Sergeant Hubbard. He told me to get back on the beat.' As he spoke his stomach rumbled and he muttered an apology. 'Been a long morning.' He sighed. 'I came in early when I heard the super on the news. Only had half my breakfast. Now it looks as if I'll be lucky to get any lunch.'

'Do you have a watchman?' Deepbriar asked, once the constable had gone.

'Yes, but he doesn't come into the offices. He patrols outside regularly during the night, but he wouldn't go between the building and the wall. To be honest, we wouldn't have a watchman at all if it wasn't for the flammable

19

chemicals we use.'

'He ought to be earning his keep on a Friday night, when the payroll is here,' Deepbriar advised. 'You might want to think about changing his routine, and make sure he includes that alleyway in his rounds.'

'We'll have to clear it first,' Pearce said, 'it's choked up with brambles. Will you be looking for fingerprints?'

'Assuming it's the same man who did the other jobs around town, he'll have been careful not to leave any,' Deepbriar said, 'but I'll check.'

There was a soft knock at the door and a girl put her head in. 'Mr Pearce?' she said timidly. 'The police station is on the telephone, asking to speak to a Constable Deepbriar.'

'That you, Deepbriar?' Hubbard's voice boomed down the line. 'We've got the superintendent asking why the CID office is unmanned when we've got a major crisis on our hands. You'd better get back here at the double.'

Having written the preliminary report on the break-in at Robertson's, Deepbriar took tea to Hubbard and the uniformed constable in the hope of learning something useful.

News had filtered through from the searchers on the moor; the suspect car and its

20

occupants had been found, and eliminated from the enquiries into Janey Smithers's disappearance. Accepting his steaming mug, Hubbard unbent enough to tell Deepbriar that the volunteers had been sent home; half the police officers would continue searching for the car, while the rest conducted house-to-house enquiries near Janey Smithers's home.

'Gough not arrived yet?' Chief Inspector Stubbs queried, coming into the office a few minutes later, with Jakes on his heels.

'No,' Deepbriar replied. 'Cup of tea, sir? You missed the trolley, but I can fetch one.'

'Best suggestion I've heard all day,' Stubbs replied. 'Anything happened here?'

Wordlessly Deepbriar handed over his report concerning the break-in at Robertson's, mouthing a silent 'tea?' at Sergeant Jakes as he headed for the door, and getting an enthusiastic nod in return.

'No good news then?' Deepbriar asked, once the chief inspector had withdrawn into his own room, and he and Jakes were alone.

Something resembling a smile twisted the sergeant's lips. 'At any other time it would have been funny, but nobody's laughing today. It took us all morning to find that car. Turns out it belongs to a businessman from Derling. He and his secretary had pitched a tent in an old quarry, and they were enjoying a bit of a private party.' Jakes grimaced.

'Just his bad luck, choosing the wrong day. He had the shock of his life when a dozen cops surrounded his love nest. His conscience was already troubling him, I reckon. Evidently he'd told his wife he was going to a meeting in Manchester.'

'He'll not be cheating on her again for a while,' Deepbriar surmised.

'No. And I don't think his secretary will agree to any more camping trips either.' Jakes took a deep draught of tea. 'I didn't realize I was so dry. I gather our petty-cash thief has been at it again.'

'Yes, odd isn't it?' Deepbriar mused. 'He left the place so neat and tidy you'd hardly know he'd been there. If it hadn't been for a brooch that was left in a drawer for safe keeping, you could count his loot in shillings and pence. Why go to all that trouble?'

'Search me.' Jakes drained his mug and got to his feet. 'I'd better get on, I've got to start going through the records. Since it doesn't look as if we're going to find this beggar the easy way, we have to trawl amongst the local perverts, looking for likely suspects. I don't know, it was hard enough when they just lurked around in the bushes, but now they're using cars I can't see we've got much chance.' He shook his head ruefully. 'It doesn't bear thinking about, does it? That poor little kid.'

A drizzly rain added to Deepbriar's depression as he pedalled home. Cold and damp, he called out from the doormat, as he stooped to remove his bicycle clips.

'Mary?' There was nobody in the kitchen, and the fire in the living room wasn't lit. 'Mary?' Deepbriar took the stairs two at a time. His wife met him at the bedroom door, and he came to an abrupt halt, feet skidding on the landing runner. 'Are you all right?'

'Yes, of course I am,' she replied, but there were telltale pink patches on her cheeks, and her eyes were slightly puffy. 'I was just putting the ironing away.'

'Something's upset you.' Deepbriar put his arms around her, a little diffident, as he had been ever since her pregnancy became obvious.

'It's nothing,' she said, pushing him away when she realized how wet his clothes were. 'You're soaked. Go and get changed and I'll put the kettle on. The steak and kidney pie's in the oven, I've only got to do the vegetables.'

'You've been listening to the news,' Deepbriar said accusingly. 'You know it upsets you...'

'No, Bella came round. Poor Bella, you can't blame her for talking about it, she was so upset. That poor little girl, imagine how her mother's feeling.'

'Don't,' Deepbriar said, stripping off his

23

damp jacket. 'Bad things happen, love. You know what Doctor Smythe said about making yourself ill. It's no use worrying about what can't be helped. Bella Emerson's an interfering old busybody; she shouldn't have come here bothering you.'

His wife sniffed, tears welling in her eyes again. 'It's not her fault. I know it's silly, all this crying, but I just can't seem to stop myself.'

Deepbriar dragged on a cardigan and led her gently to the stairs. 'Tea,' he said. 'You can have a sit down while I peel the potatoes.'

'I can do that,' she protested. 'You've been at work all day.'

'I've only been behind a desk, most of the time,' Deepbriar said and, to take her mind off the missing child, he told her about his visit to the paintworks. 'This villain never leaves anything to go on,' he said, 'but if he's such a clever thief, why doesn't he go for the wages or something?'

Mary listened, but she seemed distracted, and in the end, the potatoes and cabbage having been put on to boil, Deepbriar poured himself a cup of tea and sat down opposite her at the kitchen table. 'What's up? This isn't just to do with what Bella told you, is it?'

She shook her head. 'I'm sorry, but I can't help worrying about the house. Suppose the baby comes, and we still haven't found anywhere to live?'

24

Thorny looked across at her. 'I've been thinking the same thing, love, but there's nothing to rent in Minecliff, not that we can afford.'

'We could take Charles up on his offer of a cottage,' she said. Major Charles Brightman was heir to Minediff Manor, and currently managing the estate for his father. Despite the difference in their social positions, he and Thorny had been close friends since childhood.

'We've been over this. Moving into an estate cottage would only be a stopgap. We need a proper home.' Deepbriar ran a hand over his hair; they had already extended their tenure far beyond the norm, and should have left as soon as a new village bobby was appointed in his place. Now they only had two weeks before they had to quit Minecliff's police house. 'I know time's getting short, but I'd hate being beholden to Charles. We could afford to rent one of those little places we saw in Falbrough.'

Mary said nothing, but she placed a hand on the swelling under her apron. He knew what she was thinking: her sister and most of her friends lived in Minecliff. This village was their home, and this was where she wanted to bring up their baby.

Deepbriar sighed. There was no help for it, he would have to swallow his pride. 'All right,' he said, with forced cheerfulness, 'I'll go up to the manor after we've eaten. I suppose there's no reason a man can't be friends with his landlord.'

'As far as Charles is concerned I don't think it will make any difference,' Mary said. She reached into her pocket and pulled out a small jewellery box. Opening it, she showed him a delicate gold-wire bracelet. 'When you go, will you take this to Elaine? When she came to help fit my dress, we were talking about *something borrowed* for Saturday. I couldn't find this then, but when I described it she thought it sounded perfect.'

He nodded, trying not to look glum; he wasn't looking forward to acting as best man at Charles's and Elaine's wedding, but he didn't want Mary adding his fears to her worries.

'Thorny?' Mary laid a hand gently on his arm. 'That little girl – was there any news at all before you left? Do you think they might find her soon?'

There was no need for him to reply, his expression was answer enough.

'It makes our worries look so small and unimportant, doesn't it,' she said sadly.

Chapter Two

It hadn't been the sound of the howling wind that drove Deepbriar from bed soon after five. He had given up the attempt to sleep in the early hours. After lying wakeful for a long time, staring into the darkness with his mind churning, he had at last crept downstairs to find solace in a cup of tea. An hour later he left the house, having written Mary a note. She wouldn't like it; his wife had become very superstitious and she didn't like him to leave without the customary kiss on the cheek.

Deepbriar turned on to the Falbrough road in the predawn chill. The gale was blowing from behind him here, and the wind sent him bowling along at nearly twice his normal speed. He would be in the office long before he was due to start his morning shift, but everybody would be working extra hours until the missing girl was found.

To distract himself from dwelling on Janey Smithers's probable fate, Deepbriar pondered on his meeting with Charles Brightman the previous evening. This did nothing to lighten his mood. His friend had seemed distracted. Thorny was afraid that his earlier

27

proposal to rent them a cottage hadn't been intended as a serious offer.

Drifts of fallen leaves scuttled along the road, more than keeping pace with him, although some of them swirled, crisp and rustling, under his wheels. Dawn was approaching. With the coming of the light the wind began to abate a little; it looked as if it would become a fine day, but Deepbriar was hardly aware of his surroundings. The patchwork of golden stubble fields and green pastures passed him by, their beauty unnoticed.

The honk of a car horn sounded loud and impudent from behind him, and Deepbriar, immersed in his private gloom, was shocked into a swerve. He came to a halt, turning with a scowl on his face, and was surprised to see an elderly grey Humber pulling in at the side of the road. It was Colonel Brightman's car, but the old man didn't drive much these days; becoming frail and enjoying his retirement, he hardly ever left the manor since his son had taken over responsibility for running the estate. However, it was even more of a surprise to see Charles fling open the driver's door and come hurrying towards him.

'Thorny, you set off so early I missed you. We need to talk.'

'We're going to be busy with this manhunt all day,' Deepbriar replied stiffly, faintly annoyed at being shaken from his reverie, even though it had been a dismal one.

'I guessed that. I borrowed this old bus so I could carry your bike,' Charles said. 'Give me a hand to tie it on. I'm taking you back home, Mary has to hear this as well.'

'She might not even be awake,' Thorny protested.

'She was up and dressed when I called at the door five minutes ago,' Charles replied. 'Come on, you're wasting time.'

There was a pot of tea waiting for them in the kitchen of the police house. Mary turned from setting out the cups and greeted Charles with a smile. 'He came, then,' she said, giving her husband a look that made him squirm; she must have been awake when he left.

'I came,' Thorny said, deceiving neither of them by putting on his best authoritative manner, 'but I can't stay long.'

'I'll get straight to it,' Charles said, warily sipping his scalding tea. 'I didn't want to say anything last night until I'd made a couple of telephone calls. The answer to your problem has been staring us in the face. Mrs Twyford's cottage goes up for auction on Friday. It's small, but it would do for three of you, just about. By the time the baby needs its own room you could sort out that bit on the end that used to be a cowshed. The roof beams are rotten, but the walls are sound. It would make a perfect bathroom, and you could build a bedroom for junior up above.'

Thorny gave his friend a puzzled look. 'But we aren't looking for a place to buy.'

'Why not? You must have a bit put away. I'd be happy to give you a loan to cover the rest. We could draw up a proper agreement,' he added quickly, seeing Deepbriar's frown, 'or you could go to the bank if you don't fancy borrowing from me.' Charles grinned. 'You're a reputable character with a good steady job, Thorny, you're not exactly a high risk proposition.'

'I'm not going hundreds of pounds into debt,' Deepbriar protested. He glanced at Mary, and was surprised to see the intent expression on her face; it seemed she was taking this proposal seriously.

'It won't be that much money. I told you, I had a word with some people in the know. A cottage like that could go for less than a hundred pounds. It's small, and there's no indoor plumbing except the tap in the kitchen. Whoever buys it will have a lot of work to do.'

'But the baby's due in a few weeks,' Deepbriar objected, picturing the tiny little privy at the bottom of the garden. It had come as a surprise when he'd realized just how primitive the place was. Mrs Twyford had been a wealthy woman, nice, but a bit of an oddity.

Having no close relatives after her husband's death, she had left her estate to the parish of Minecliff.

'I could manage,' Mary said abruptly. 'Plenty of women cope with having babies without the luxury of an indoor toilet. My mother had four of us.'

'I don't see why the bathroom couldn't be done quickly,' Charles said airily. 'It's only a matter of putting on a new roof, and a bit of plumbing.'

'It would still cost a fair bit. You're talking as if we'd get the place for nothing,' Deepbriar countered.

'I told you, it could be a real bargain,' Charles said. 'And you won't know if you don't try. Come on, Thorny, where's your sense of adventure?'

'I never had one; you're confusing me with you.' Deepbriar rubbed a hand over the back of his neck. 'I suppose it wouldn't hurt to see how much money we can put together.'

The first smile he had seen on Mary's face for a long time seemed to light up the whole room. 'I've been holding on to my Co-op dividend for years,' she said, 'without really knowing why. And we've got our savings in the post office. Thorny, just think of it! Our own house! If it helps, we could sell grandfather's clock; you've always hated it, and I wouldn't mind letting it go in a good cause. Bella told me she'd seen one like it in a shop

31

in Belston, and they were asking twenty-five pounds! Imagine, that's almost a quarter of what we'd need to buy the cottage.'

Chief Inspector Stubbs walked into the yard as Thorny lifted his bike from the back of the elderly Humber. He was still fifteen minutes early, but noting that his boss looked mildly disapproving, Deepbriar hurried to put his bicycle away. Unabashed, Charles wound up the rope they'd used to anchor the bike, sketched a salute and offered the senior detective a breezy 'Good morning,' before leaping back into the driving seat and pulling out of the yard.

'Sorry I wasn't here earlier, sir,' Deepbriar said, holding the door open.

'No, you're not late,' Stubbs said. 'I was only thinking it's time you stopped relying on two wheels; a bike is fine for a village bobby, but you're a CID man now. I've asked Jakes to teach you to drive. Once the current panic is over you can do it during working hours.'

'Yes sir,' Deepbriar said gloomily. He'd had a provisional licence for some time but he didn't care much for cars; his previous experiences behind the wheel had been laughable.

'Morning, Chief Inspector; morning, Thorny,' Sergeant Parsons nodded a greeting as the two men approached the front

32

desk. 'Chief Superintendent Murray has arrived. He wants everyone to gather in the canteen.' He lowered his voice so only Deepbriar could hear. 'Lots of talk and not much action,' he predicted.

In the crowded canteen the chief super-intendent from Cawster CID signalled for everyone to relax as the officers stood to attention. He wasted no time in coming to the point. 'As you know, Janey Smithers is still missing. Since we have our hands full in Cawster with a couple of other serious crimes, we're looking to Falbrough to take on some of the workload. You'll be concentrating your efforts on finding the car. The witness said it was old, but I don't want you to rely on that too much. Evidently his eyesight's not what it might be; he could have made a mistake. You'll also be questioning all the known villains involved with messing about with little girls in the past, and any dodgy characters who are suspected of being that way inclined.' He looked at Stubbs. 'That will be your department, Chief Inspector. Obviously we're asking all the adjoining forces for their cooperation, since we can't rule out the possibility that this man isn't local.

'For the moment we're concentrating the main thrust of our search around Falbrough because of the similarity of this case and the disappearance of Miriam Pitt, six years ago. You won't need reminding that she too was believed to have been forced into a car, and that her body was found in Falbrough woods, only two miles from here. Let's hope history isn't about to repeat itself, but just in case, the dog teams will be deployed there today. I'm sure you also don't need reminding that the man who killed Miriam was never found.'

Half an hour later, Chief Inspector Stubbs called Deepbriar into his office. Every other CID officer had already been given a job, and Thorny had begun to think he'd been overlooked.

'Did you get involved in the Miriam Pitt case, Thorny?' Stubbs asked.

Deepbriar shook his head. 'No sir.'

'I see. So, you're coming to this fresh, as it were. Listen, I want you to get down to the records room and take a look at the file on the Miriam Pitt case. And ask Sergeant Parsons about any other incidents he thinks might be connected, even ones that weren't seen as important at the time. He's got a good memory for that sort of thing.'

'Sir?' Deepbriar was baffled. 'I thought Sergeant Jakes was already looking into the likely villains on this patch.'

'He is. You can leave our known offenders to him. What I want from you is a fresh approach. It's a long shot, but you might just come up with something.'

All Deepbriar came up with in the next

34

three hours was a growing ache behind his eyes. He had read every scrap of information in the file on the Miriam Pitt case, and he could see why Chief Superintendent Murray suspected a connection with Janey Smithers's abduction; not only had both of them been snatched from Cawster in late autumn, but the girls were both fair-haired, of approximately the same age.

There had been no direct witnesses to Miriam's kidnapping. She had called briefly at her aunt's house after school; leaving there for home, she had apparently vanished off the face of the earth. Her brother, a boy of thirteen, had set off on the same journey only five minutes later, and he had seen no sign of his sister, although he had expected to catch up with her. At first it had been hoped that she was merely lost, but the speed with which she had disappeared suggested otherwise; right from the start, Cawster CID had suspected foul play. All speculation had ended when her body was discovered.

Deepbriar returned the file to its place, returned to the front desk and told Sergeant Parsons about his quest. 'I dunno,' the sergeant grumbled. 'Six years? Who's to say I can remember anything after all that time? What am I supposed to be, some sort of vaudeville act? Just call me Mister Blooming Memory Man.'

'Everybody knows you've got the best

memory in Falbrough, Sarge,' Deepbriar coaxed.

'Humph,' Parsons replied. 'Maybe there was something. I'll put my thinking cap on while I'm eating lunch, all right?'

Deepbriar thanked him, and took himself off to the canteen, where a doorstep cheese-and-pickle sandwich and a cup of strong tea dealt with the headache. Reporting back to the CID office half an hour later, he found Chief Inspector Stubbs waiting for him, a piece of paper in his hand. 'Ah, there you are, Thorny.'

'I'm afraid I haven't turned up anything yet,' Deepbriar began, but his superior cut him short.

'Never mind that now, I've got another job for you. We're getting so many reports of likely cars that we can't keep up with them all, but I think this one might be worth looking into. A large black saloon was seen entering the forestry plantation early this morning, near Holgate. We checked with the forester, and whoever it is has no business up there. You'll find Sergeant Jakes in the yard; I suggested he should take you with him on this one, because it might give you a chance to get behind the wheel, once you're off the public road.'

Deepbriar had been in a car with Jakes once before, and he hadn't enjoyed it. This second trip with the sergeant at the wheel was enough to persuade him that Chief Inspector Stubbs was right; he needed to get a full licence as soon as possible. By the time they arrived in Holgate Thorny's hand was painfully cramped, so tight had been his grip upon the strap that hung on the inside of the door.

'Any idea where we go from here?' Jakes asked, slowing down to walking pace, and blithely unaware of Deepbriar's discomfort.

'That lane by the war memorial,' Deepbriar said, unclenching his jaw muscles.

'Right. Look, Thorny, I know Mr Stubbs said you were to do a bit of driving, but I think we'd better wait until after we've tracked this bloke down, if that's all right by you.'

Deepbriar nodded, more relieved than otherwise. Taking over the driving might prevent their being involved in a high-speed accident, but they'd be unlikely to catch up with their villain if he couldn't get the car out of first gear.

The daylight seemed to fade as they drove into the forest, rank upon rank of conifers towering over them on both sides, the lane getting ever narrower, and bordered on each side by a high wire fence.

'Where the heck is the entrance?' Jakes fretted. 'Are you sure this is the right road?'

'Stop!' Deepbriar said urgently. The car screeched to a halt.

'What? Is this the wrong way?'

'No. I saw something. Through there.' He pointed at the rows of tree trunks marching up a steep hill. 'The light was reflecting off something, I think it was a car.'

Jakes reversed a few yards, and Deepbriar peered into the shadowy forest. 'Yes, black car, parked. I can't see how big it is.'

'Right, let's go get him,' Jakes said enthusiastically, jabbing his foot on the accelerator.

The barrier which normally prevented entry to the forest stood open. Jakes slowed down a little to study it. 'Chain's been cut,' he reported, speeding up again. The track turned and took them along the side of the hill, and there, not 200 yards away, was the car.

'It's pretty big,' Jakes said. He drove closer, stopping where the track was too narrow to allow the other car to pass. 'A Morris. Not old, but then he could have got that wrong. And here comes our trespasser.'

From between the trees a man appeared, running flat out. Upon reaching his car he dragged open the door and flung himself into the driving seat. With a roar from the engine and a spurt of stones beneath the wheels, he tore away from them at breakneck speed. A grim expression on his face, Jakes took off in pursuit, while Thorny braced himself as best he could, clinging to the dashboard with his teeth gritted. He thought forlornly of his unborn child, and sent up a silent prayer that the baby wouldn't be orphaned before it even arrived.

The unmade road was deeply rutted in places. The police car jolted, skidding as it hit a patch of wet sawdust where a fallen tree had been cleared, and Deepbriar got an unhealthily close view of a tree trunk, looming across his side of the windscreen. Just in time Jakes wrenched the steering wheel round and straightened up. The other car was doing no better; having arrived at a fork in the road the driver seemed unable to decide which way to take, and almost came to grief as his nearside wheels spun dangerously over a steep drop. Taking advantage of the man's hesitation, Jakes gained about twenty yards on him, and reached out a hand to sound the bell.

A discordant clamour assaulted the two officers' ears, loud even over the noise of the motor. Its effect was dramatic; with a roar from the overtaxed engine and a screech of tyres, the other car fishtailed wildly, before seeming to leap across the shallow bank, all that separated the track from the steep drop towards the road, now some hundreds of feet below. Before Deepbriar even had time to blink the vehicle was gone from sight.

'Strewth!' Jakes slammed his feet to the floor, and the police car slid to a halt, narrowly missing a similar plunge down the hill. The two officers leapt from the car and dashed down the hillside, following the sounds of splintering wood and battered metal. Having somehow missed a direct collision with the trees, the car scraped its way between two closely packed rows of trunks, its progress gradually arrested by scrub and saplings. It came to rest at last with its radiator wrapped around a protruding rock. The boot sprang open, the engine died, and abruptly there was no sound in the wood except the tick of cooling metal.

'Well, we got lucky,' Jakes breathed, as the dented door opened as far as the surrounding trees would permit, and a man began struggling to get out. 'He's alive.' He sprinted the last few yards. 'Police,' he called. 'Stay where you are.'

'Look out!' Deepbriar yelled. The man, half-in and half-out of the car, delivered a well-aimed punch at the sergeant's solar plexus, and Jakes fell back, winded.

The man still hadn't quite extricated himself from the wreck when Deepbriar reached him, but it wouldn't take a moment for him to win free. Fists clenched, he began to launch himself in the constable's direction. 'Bloody coppers, you're...' the man began, but the words ended in a screech. Deepbriar had grabbed the half-open door and done his best to slam it shut. The miscreant slumped back into his seat, clutching at his arm.

Jakes rose to his feet, his face pale. Without a word he pulled a pair of handcuffs from his pocket. Between them the two officers hauled the man from the car and secured his wrists. Their captive was a burly figure, with thick, greying hair. A streak of blood was oozing from a cut on the top of his head, but he didn't seem to be seriously hurt.

'Well, that takes the biscuit,' Deepbriar said, grinning as the man scowled at him. 'We've caught ourselves a very slippery villain, Sergeant. Did you notice his luggage?'

'I can't say I did.' Taking a look as they led their prisoner back up the hill, Jakes recoiled at the sight that met his eyes. The boot was full of bloody joints of meat.

'No point taking the bits that won't sell,' Deepbriar said, 'butcher them where they drop and they're easier to carry, isn't that right, Mr Beenham?'

This brought only an obscenity by way of reply.

'Let's get him back to the car,' Deepbriar suggested, tightening his grip on their prisoner's arm. 'The sooner he's behind bars the better.'

Jakes rubbed his bruised midriff with his free hand. 'I couldn't agree more. Of course, if we really want him subdued, you could take the wheel for the drive home,' he added, his lips quirking as he gave the constable a sidelong glance.

'No need, Sergeant, I reckon you'll do a better job than me,' Deepbriar retorted. 'You may not have noticed, but my guardian angel's been working overtime; I gave myself up for lost long ago.'

Chapter Three

The arrest of Clive Beenham, a rogue who had plagued the constabulary for years, brought with it a lightening of the mood at Falbrough's police station, and an illogical hope that their luck might have changed. The next day officers came on duty with a spring in their step, attacking their work with a new enthusiasm, as if pure dedication would ensure that Janey Smithers was found unscathed.

This brief euphoria didn't last. On Wednesday morning Deepbriar reported for duty with his eyes sticky from lack of sleep. Having reached home at eleven the night before, crawled into bed and slept for less than three hours before insomnia claimed him once more, he was finding it hard to be optimistic. The full force of the county constabulary was being thrown into the search for the missing child. All leave and rest days had been cancelled, and the enquiry was being pursued with the utmost urgency, yet they seemed to be making no progress.

Deepbriar had left Mary in a tearful mood again. Even reminding her that the auction was only two days away failed to lift her spirits. They had managed to put together the sum of £105, which Charles Brightman assured them should be enough to buy Mrs Twyford's cottage, but Deepbriar couldn't help reflecting that their efforts would be wasted if he couldn't take time off to attend the auction.

Hearing that Chief Inspector Stubbs was already in his office, Deepbriar knocked on the door, feeling unaccountably nervous as he waited for the invitation to enter.

'Morning, Thorny.' Stubbs looked tired and drawn. Deepbriar knew that the man had twin daughters, a year older than Janey Smithers. The chief inspector was taking this case hard, and he wasn't the only one.

'Sir. I'd like your permission to go to Cawster,' Deepbriar said, without preamble. 'Sergeant Parsons has a vague idea about a rumour that was going the rounds years ago, something that happened not long before the Miriam Pitt case. He can't recall any details, but I thought it might be relevant. I want to go and look through their records.'

Stubbs rubbed his forehead, as if there was a pain between his eyes. There was a pause before he answered, 'Yes, whatever you think, Deepbriar, but we'd better clear it with Chief Superintendent Murray; although he's practically turned the case over to me, I mustn't tread on any toes at headquarters. He'll be calling in shortly. I'll ask him.'

'Thank you, sir.' Feeling unable to broach the subject of the auction on Friday in the face of Stubbs's obvious abstraction, Deepbriar saluted and turned on his heel, cursing his cowardice as he pulled the door shut.

The chief superintendent arrived within minutes. Ignoring Deepbriar, who had risen to his feet with a brisk 'Good morning, sir', Murray charged past and into Stubbs's room without bothering to announce his arrival, slamming the door behind him. Deepbriar sighed, reaching for the file on the Pitt case. He almost knew every document by heart. The conversation between the two senior officers could be heard as an indistinguishable murmur, until suddenly, with great clarity, Murray's voice reached his ears.

'I need all your available men on the ground! Don't forget that note on Deepbriar's record...'

Here Stubbs must have interrupted, but a moment later Murray's booming tones rang out again. 'Be that as it may, I still don't see why you were so keen to take on an aging village constable. At his time of life you can't turn the man into a detective. And another thing: all leave's been cancelled, but I see he's been signed off for the day on Saturday.'

With his cheeks flushing hotly Deepbriar

45

rose from his chair, intent on leaving before he heard any more; he was very glad none of the other CID officers were there. A minute later Stubbs found Deepbriar standing in the corridor, studying an out of date duty roster on the notice board. The chief inspector raised his eyebrows and tilted his head towards the office. Without a word Deepbriar followed him back inside.

'Chief Superintendent Murray has asked why you need the day off on Saturday, Constable,' Stubbs said, once Deepbriar was standing at attention before his desk.

'I'm due to act as best man at a friend's wedding, sir,' Deepbriar replied. 'He asked me a long time ago. In view of the current crisis I was planning to work a double shift on Sunday to make up the time.'

'This person who's getting married, is he a colleague?' Murray barked.

'No sir, but we've known each other since we were children. I wouldn't like to let him down, not at such short notice.'

'He may not be a police officer, but he is a bit of a local hero,' Stubbs put in.

'You know him, Chief Inspector?' Murray sounded surprised.

'Only slightly, sir. Major Brightman has a very distinguished war record.'

'Brightman? From Minecliff Manor?' If he'd been surprised before, the chief superintendent looked positively amazed at this

46

revelation, staring at Deepbriar as if he'd just dropped in through the roof.

'Yes sir,' Deepbriar returned woodenly. He was used to this reaction; village bobbies weren't supposed to mix socially with the landed gentry.

'Boyhood friends, eh?' Murray became positively avuncular. 'Well, Constable, that merits special consideration. You're right, you can't let Major Brightman down.'

'Thank you, sir.'

'And I take it Deepbriar can pop over to Cawster to look at some records today,' Stubbs prompted. 'You did ask my department to look into possible suspects in the area.'

'Very well. Sergeant Foster will see you get whatever you need, Constable.' He gave a nod of dismissal and Deepbriar escaped, hurrying past the newly arrived Sergeant Jakes with a perfunctory greeting. After the encounter with Chief Superintendent Murray he felt the need of solitude and fresh air.

He didn't enjoy either for long. The bus from Falbrough to Cawster was crowded. Choosing to travel upstairs, although he didn't smoke, Deepbriar peered through the swirl of fumes at the passing countryside. He felt a twinge of nostalgia for his old job. At this time of day he would be setting off on his beat: once round Minecliff on foot,

47

then a cycle ride through the peaceful lanes to the neighbouring villages. More important, he would have little contact with senior officers like the chief superintendent. He gave himself a mental shake. There was a price to pay for being in the CID; he was a detective now, and if he was to convince Murray that he was worthy of the title, he had to unearth something useful.

With fresh determination he turned his thoughts to what Parsons had told him; the sergeant had an old-fashioned copper's instincts, as well as a memory rivalling that of the proverbial elephant. The rumour circulating years ago, around twelve months before Miriam Pitt disappeared, suggested that a man had tried to coax two girls into his car. For some reason the affair had been swept under the carpet. If that was true, it was unlikely that the official records would tell him anything; he needed to tap into the station's grapevine.

By midday Deepbriar knew he'd been right; there was nothing of any significance to be found in the records. He went to the canteen, collected shepherd's pie with carrots and cabbage from the counter, and looked around for an old acquaintance, so he could begin the serious business of the day.

Constable Peters was downing the last of his apple crumble when Deepbriar abandoned small talk and came to the point. Peters shook his head, denying all knowledge of the rumour. 'Come on, Thorny, nobody would have withheld information that might have helped us find Miriam Pitt. We all feel the same when a kid's involved.'

Deepbriar pulled his roly-poly pudding towards him; it looked a bit stodgy and unappetizing, drowned in lumpy custard. He sighed; he missed his home-cooked meals. 'So how do you think this story about an attempted abduction got started?'

'Probably just a mix-up. Plenty of children run off and then turn up safe and well after a night or two camping out in a shed. Somebody could have got the wrong end of the stick.' Peters stood up, stacking his crockery on a tray. 'If you've got nothing better to do, we're flipping short-handed. I'll be walking the south-eastern beat as well as my own this afternoon.'

'Sorry, I'm done with bashing pavements,' Deepbriar replied. 'It's my brain that does the work now.'

'Humph. With no exercise you'll soon be too fat to get into the uniform anyway.' Peters stomped away, and two younger constables came to join Deepbriar as he chewed on his unappetizing pudding, intent on twitting him about his move to CID. Neither of them had been based at Cawster seven years before, and when he mentioned the rumour it was plain they had no idea what he was talking about.

Cutting his lunch-break short, Deepbriar returned to the general office. Sergeant Riley had taken over the enquiry desk, and as soon as the man was alone Deepbriar approached him, repeating the question he had put to Peters.

'You what? Are you crazy?' Riley had never been a man to mince words, and he glared at Deepbriar, leaning over the desk, his beetle-brows drawn into a deep black slash. Since he'd been known to quell a near riot single-handedly and without a blow being landed, Deepbriar felt a stirring of unease.

'I'm not making accusations,' Deepbriar said. 'All I heard is, this rumour was going the rounds, back in 1950. I just wondered if you knew where it started.'

'I don't know and I don't care. It's a lot of bloody nonsense.' Riley put his face uncomfortably close to Deepbriar's. 'You go spreading that kind of tittle-tattle, when every man here's working his fanny off to find this missing kid, and you're likely to get yourself in trouble, Mr Detective Constable. Now get out of here and let me get on with my job.'

Holding up his hands in a gesture of submission, Deepbriar withdrew, returning to the canteen where he sat hunched over a belated cup of tea. There were still a few officers finishing their lunch, including Sergeant Foster, but he got the impression they were all avoiding him. He chewed on his bottom lip, staring into space. Riley's reaction struck him as excessive. Of course, everyone was tired and on edge with all the extra hours they were working, but there had been something defensive about the big man's response, and an expression in his eyes that suggested Deepbriar might have come too close to the truth.

Half an hour later his suspicions seemed well-founded. He was called to the telephone. Stubbs was on the line, sounding even wearier than he had that morning.

'What have you been up to, Deepbriar? I've just had a lecture from the DCI over there. He says you'll be slung out on your ear if you carry on the way you're going. It was all I could do to persuade him not to mention it to the chief superintendent. I get the impression you've seriously upset somebody.'

'You could say that,' Deepbriar replied cautiously, eyeing the three officers within earshot, all of them keeping their heads lowered assiduously over their work.

'Well, I suppose you've got your reasons, but you'd better leave it for now. We can't have anyone running to Chief Superintend-

51

ent Murray telling tales. Sergeant Jakes is coming to pick you up, he's returning some files. It's an ill wind, as they say; if you take the back roads it'll give him a chance to give you your first driving lesson.'

Deepbriar's day was sliding from bad to worse. He trailed reluctantly out to the car behind Jakes a little later, refusing point blank to take the wheel until they were well away from the city centre.

'Come on, Thorny,' Jakes said, pulling up in a quiet country lane and applying the handbrake, his tone breezily encouraging, 'it's not that difficult. You'll enjoy driving once you get the hang of it. Change places, and I'll talk you through the controls.'

Deepbriar did his best, concentrating on Jakes's instructions, getting the feel of the gears and the pedals while the car was stationary, but his hands had become sticky with sweat and his breathing was laboured before he even started the motor.

'Relax,' Jakes said. 'All you're going to do is put the car into first gear and ease it forward a few yards, then brake, put it back into neutral and put the handbrake on. Couldn't be simpler. Lift your left foot a little as you press down gently with the right. Easy does it.'

The car leapt forward in a series of spine-jarring jumps, and Deepbriar slammed both feet to the floor, the engine roaring

52

because his right foot was still over the accelerator instead of the brake. Luckily, since he'd also hit the clutch, the car rolled to a halt.

'Sorry,' he muttered, snatching his feet off the pedals while the car was still in gear. With another leap and a jolt so sharp that Deepbriar was sure he felt his teeth rattle, the vehicle stalled.

'Not to worry,' Jakes said, though he sounded a little less assured than he had a moment ago. 'Listen, Thorny, driving's not that hard. I taught my kid sister last year, and if she can do it, anyone can. Come on, try again.'

Several attempts later they were fifty yards further down the road, and the jumps had become a little less violent. Hands gripping with white-knuckled intensity, Deepbriar attempted his first junction. The vehicle veered wildly on to the verge. Jakes yelped and grabbed the wheel, pulling them back on to the tarmac before they ended up in the ditch.

The sergeant was uncharacteristically silent as he drove the car back to Falbrough. Thorny reflected miserably that he was probably wondering what on earth he could say to Chief Inspector Stubbs. Luckily, there was a minor panic erupting in the office on their return, and the subject was forgotten in a flurry of activity; a black car had been found abandoned on the moors, and another search was being organized.

Pedalling home after nightfall, Deepbriar felt depression enfolding him, as dark as the cloudy autumnal sky. Little Janey was still missing. His attempts to discover the roots of Parsons's rumour had failed, and his first driving lesson had been farcical. Added to that, he could see no possibility of having time off on Friday to attend the auction, which was a problem, since Mary had set her heart on the little cottage in Stellings Lane. He had an idea it was possible for a prospective buyer who couldn't attend a sale to deposit his bid with the auctioneer, but he didn't know how that was done.

'You look worn out,' Mary said sympathetically, almost pushing him into his chair at the dining table. 'I've kept your meal warm. Unless you want a cup of tea first.'

'No, don't bother,' he replied, a little heartened by the rich aroma of beef hotpot emanating from the saucepan on the stove. 'That smells lovely.'

'I knew there was no point cooking anything that might spoil,' his wife replied, dishing up his meal and putting the plate in front of him. 'Charles and Elaine called in an hour ago. I told them you'd be late, so Charles said he'd come back about nine. I think it might be to do with the auction.'

Deepbriar merely nodded, his mouth full. As usual, his mood lifted a little as he savoured Mary's cooking; maybe things weren't so bad. With luck his friend would be able to tell him how to place his bid. He had almost finished eating when the knocker at the door sounded. His heart sank. Until they vacated the police house, Constable Giddens was still living in Falbrough, and he'd long since gone home. Deepbriar went to open the door; there were still times when he felt more like Minecliff's village bobby than a detective.

'Mr Lofthouse.' Deepbriar looked at the retired schoolmaster and resisted the temptation to heave a sigh. 'Is something wrong?'

'It's Grigsdyke,' the lean old man said. 'The noise has been very disturbing, going on for an hour at least, shouting and swearing, and things being thrown. My sister Lavinia is concerned for the children. We thought we heard one of them scream.'

There was no need for any further explanation. Alf Grigsdyke wasn't a bad sort most of the time, but on the rare occasions when he was in his cups, he became a different man.

'I'll come, but I doubt if there's much I can do,' Deepbriar said, reaching for his jacket and hat. 'You know the way it is with domestic troubles, I can knock on the door, but I've no right to go charging into his house.'

In the past he'd locked Alf up on several occasions, usually charging him with being drunk and disorderly outside the Speckled Goose; on one memorable night he'd come away from the encounter with a spectacular black eye.

All seemed quiet as they came to Bridge Lane. With a sketchy apologetic smile Mr Lofthouse opened his freshly painted front gate and hurried through it. 'I really must check that Lavinia isn't fretting,' he whispered, almost tiptoeing up the neat path. Deepbriar didn't bother to suppress his sigh this time. He turned to the Grigsdykes' house, where the front gate was long since missing and the path was overgrown with weeds.

Rapping on the door with his knuckles, Deepbriar was surprised when it swung open at his touch. 'Alf? Anybody there?' A bare light bulb shone at the top of the stairs, and beneath it sat nine-year-old Willy in outgrown pyjamas, staring down at him, wide-eyed.

'You all right, son?' Deepbriar asked. The boy nodded.

'Where's your dad?'

'In the kitchen,' came the whispered response.

'Fine. I'll go and have a word with him. You just hop back into your bed now, before you get cold.' Obediently the boy vanished, swift and silent, and Deepbriar walked warily down the hall. 'Can I come in?' he called.

He needn't have worried. Alf had reached the maudlin state that always followed his drunken bouts; on this occasion he must have started his serious drinking at midday. He sat at the kitchen table, a hunched and miserable figure, head in hands, looking up with little interest when Deepbriar entered.

'You've been making a bit of a mess,' Deepbriar remarked, stepping carefully over the remains of a milk bottle and a plate that lay in the doorway.

'It ain't my fault, Thorny,' the drunk whimpered. 'I try to stay off it, you know I do. I can't help myself.'

'Where's Mrs Grigsdkye?'

The answer was a jerk of the head towards the back door, and Deepbriar opened it, staring into the darkness. 'Mrs Grigsdyke?'

Somewhere a bolt was drawn back. Two figures emerged from the outside privy, one almost as large and dishevelled as Grigsdyke himself, the other a little slip of a girl, small for her ten years. They came wordlessly into the light spilling from the room and paused on the doorstep.

Peg Grigsdyke was a large woman, and could give as good as she got; the only time Alf had needed hospital treatment after one of his heavy bouts his injuries had been caused by his wife's rolling-pin, but standing in the doorway tonight, she looked as wary as young Willy. As for the child, her face was red and swollen with weeping, and she was clinging to her mother's hand as if her life depended upon it.

'What's been going on here, Alf?' Deepbriar demanded. His gaze skimmed the kitchen, and he noted a carving knife, lying on the table not far from Alf's hands. 'Is everything all right, Mrs Grigsdyke?'

The woman nodded briefly, coming inside and closing the door while Alf continued to moan into his hands. 'Nothing to trouble yourself about, thank you, Constable,' she said firmly. In a casual manner, she picked up the knife and slid it into a drawer. 'I'd better be getting Deirdre off to bed.' Leading the child past her prostrated husband, she went upstairs.

Deepbriar knew from past experience that it was no use talking to Alf in his present state, nevertheless he made the attempt. 'You've even had your wife worried this time, Alf,' he said. 'If I was still in uniform I'd lock you up for the night and see if that would make you see sense. You and booze don't mix, man. For your own sake, give it up.'

Grigsdyke began to sob quietly, his shoulders heaving. Deepbriar shook his head helplessly and left him to it.

When he got home, Charles was comfortably settled in Thorny's favourite armchair. 'I thought Minecliff had a new village bobby,' he said cheerfully. 'But Mary tells me you were called out to deal with the Grigsdykes' domestic troubles again.'

'Until we move out Constable Giddens is only here during the day. It was only Alf; trouble is, he never learns. He'll be full of remorse in the morning, but you can bet he'll hit the bottle again in a month or two.' Thorny lowered himself on to the settee. 'Didn't you bring Elaine with you?'

'She's in the kitchen with Mary, talking wedding cake, or flowers; I'm not sure which.'

'Well, I wanted a chance to talk to you on your own, so perhaps it's just as well. Look, Charles, there's no way I can get to the auction on Friday. All leave and rest days have been cancelled; it was all I could do to get permission to be at the wedding on Saturday. Mary's set her heart on that cottage. I mean, it's one thing if we can't afford it, but if we miss it just because I can't get time off work, she'll never forgive me.'

'Not to worry. If you'll trust me with your cash I can take care of it.' Charles Brightman leant forward to pull an envelope from his pocket. 'I came to leave this with you, but in the circumstances I'll hang on to it.'

'What is it?' Deepbriar was instantly sus-

59

picious. 'Look, Charles, we've got a hundred and five pounds, and that's it. I can't afford any more.'

'You already said how much it means to Mary. Twenty pounds, that's all this is, Thorny, but it might make all the difference. I told you, if you need to use it we can have a proper loan agreement written up, and you can pay it off at two bob a week, complete with interest. It's no worse than paying rent, and the place will be completely yours in a few years. With luck this won't be necessary. We're not going to fall out, are we?'

'I suppose not,' Deepbriar grumbled. 'But don't you go one penny higher than a hundred and twenty-five!'

'I promise,' Charles said. 'Just leave it to me.' He smiled. 'Mary was telling us about the arrest you made. Are you still taking the flak over it?'

'Oh yes, I shan't live that down in a hurry. After nearly twenty years as a village copper, when I finally make it to plain clothes, the first villain I nab is a poacher.' Deepbriar did his best to hide a yawn, and his friend rose to his feet.

'It looks as if you need your bed. I'll go and gather up Elaine. Don't worry, Thorny, that cottage is as good as yours. Keep your chin up and look on the bright side, like my old man always says.'

60

Deepbriar nodded. He wouldn't destroy Brightman's ebullient mood by reminding him about the missing child, but he would be lucky if his own sleep wasn't troubled by nightmares again.

Chapter Four

It was late on Thursday afternoon when a police dog called Rebel found a child's shoe. Rebel's handler had finished his allotted duties, but he was in the habit of letting the dog have a free run before returning home, as a reward for a day's hard work. This time he chose to stop at a long-abandoned quarry on the outskirts of Falbrough, taking the opportunity to smoke a quiet cigarette while the dog bounded away from him. The place was a wilderness of deep craters, pocked by the burrows of small animals. In summer the hills and holes would be head-high with nettles, but the plants had died back to a sad brown mat as winter approached. Rebel had only been gone a couple of minutes when he began to bark.

The shoe was identified by Janey's parents, and the search at the old quarry was intensified, but nothing further was found. It had been dark for several hours when the searchers headed wearily and disconsolately home. Cycling the lonely lanes, totally unaware of his surroundings, Deepbriar was lost in morbid thoughts. The world suddenly seemed an alien and unfriendly place; how could any man harm a child?

As he approached the house, plodding slowly from the shed to the kitchen door, Deepbriar tried to drag himself out of his misery; Mary wasn't to be allowed to worry, not in her delicate state.

In the event, she was the one who cured his despondency. When he walked in, she took one look at his face and came to put her arms around him. 'Oh, Thorny. Have they found her?'

'Not yet. One of her shoes turned up, though. It doesn't look good, love.' He returned her hug. 'I'm sorry, I don't want you getting upset.'

To his surprise she didn't cry. 'There's still a chance that things will turn out all right,' she said. 'And if they don't, well, tragedies happen all over the place, all the time, and we can't let ourselves get upset over every one of them, or none of us would ever have any peace.' She freed herself from his grasp, looking sad, but much more like her old self. 'I'll put the kettle on, and we'll be selfish and think about ourselves for a while. Life goes on. Tomorrow we'll be trying to buy our very own house, and on Saturday Elaine is getting married to Charles. After giving up hope, it looks as if we might have the family we always wanted, and that's best of all. Good things happen too, thank heavens.'

Thorny sighed, feeling some of the stiffness ease out of his shoulders. 'You're right. I'm glad you're seeing things that way, because I shan't be able to get to the auction tomorrow. You don't have to worry about the cottage, though. I gave the money to Charles last night, and he's going in my place. I'm sorry, but it's one of those things. I'd have had to cry off being best man on Saturday if the chief super wasn't such a snob.'

'I wondered what was going on between the two of you.' Mary gave a decisive nod. 'I'd have bid for the cottage myself, if I had to.'

'Reckon you would.' Deepbriar grinned, reaching to squeeze her hand, hugely relieved to see his wife's usual spirit resurfacing after the weeks of depression. 'It's probably just as well you don't have to, though; the excitement could have made Deepbriar junior turn up early.'

The next day, with the hunt for Janey Smithers at full pitch again, Deepbriar had no time to think about the auction. He'd only been in the office a few minutes when he was summoned to join a large group of officers, both uniformed and CID, who were to begin yet more house-to-house enquiries and conduct a further search in and around the quarry where the shoe had been found. A dozen men had been brought in from Cawster to help, under the watchful eye of

Sergeant Riley. While they were all waiting for teams to be organized, Chief Superintendent Murray arrived, and spent several minutes with the senior officers on the case before heading back towards his car. For some reason he noticed Deepbriar, standing a little way from the other men, and he came across to join him.

'Morning, Constable. Big day tomorrow, eh? Is the ceremony being held in the cathedral?'

'No sir, they decided on the village church,' Deepbriar said. 'Just a quiet affair.'

'Really? Oh well, each to their own. It's good to have something to celebrate when we're in the middle of all this, eh?' The man sketched a smile, probably priding himself on this show of condescension. 'Convey my best wishes to the bride and groom, won't you?'

At that instant Deepbriar noticed that Sergeant Riley was watching this exchange with a look of profound concern; he couldn't possibly have heard what was being said. The chance was too good to miss. Giving the chief superintendent an earnest look, Deepbriar nodded vigorously, as though pleased with such an important man's attention. 'Yes sir,' he said, a little more loudly than necessary. 'Thank you sir, thank you very much. I'll do that.'

Only slightly bemused by the constable's

response, the head of the county CID returned to his car. Deepbriar walked across to Riley. 'May I have a word, Sergeant?'

Riley nodded and followed him, unexpectedly meek. They climbed a steep bank of spoil, sufficiently far from the other men to be out of earshot. Deepbriar wasted no time. 'I know you're hiding something,' he said. 'You can tell me, here and now, or next time I see Murray I'll suggest he has a word with you instead of leaving it to me. If that happens, the whole thing will come out. It'll be official.'

'Are you threatening me, Constable?' Riley scowled.

'Depends how you look at it, Sergeant,' Deepbriar said woodenly. He knew he was taking a risk, but he was sure he was on the right track.

'You don't know a thing.' Sergeant Riley turned, as if ready to walk away.

'I know the damage a black mark can do to a man's record,' Deepbriar shot back feelingly, 'even when there's no grounds for it.'

'Look, if I fill you in on what happened, can you keep my name out of it?'

The constable pretended to consider this proposition. 'I'll do my best,' he said, taking out his notebook. 'Let's have it.'

There was no time to follow up the information that he'd scribbled down at the quarry;

questioning local householders was always a slow job, and when Deepbriar eventually arrived back at Falbrough he was greeted by Sergeant Jakes, who was putting his coat and hat on. 'Just in time, Thorny,' Jakes said, cheerfully, grabbing him by the arm and leading him outside again. 'When I told Stubbs I didn't want to tackle this on my own, he said I could take any company I could find. Lucky he didn't know you were on your way back, or he'd never have been so rash.'

Deepbriar consulted his watch. 'It's gone two o'clock,' he protested. 'I've not had a bite to eat since seven.'

'There's a bag of barley sugars in the car, they'll keep you going for a bit.' Jakes delivered a friendly jab to his older colleague's well padded ribs. 'You could live off your fat for a week if you had to.'

They drove to a house in Derling, where they spent an hour questioning a man convicted of molesting children many years before. After that they trailed around half the county, checking that the suspect's alibi for the previous Sunday was watertight, before speeding back to Falbrough, with Deepbriar's stomach rumbling audibly the whole way. By this time the canteen had nothing on offer but some dried-up cheese sandwiches and a tired sausage roll, all of which Deepbriar devoured, washing the unpalatable

67

mouthfuls down with several pints of tea.

The afternoon was over, but the station was still busy, a buzz and a stir filling it, reminding the constable of a wasps' nest, recently stirred with a stick. Deepbriar found Stubbs in his office. The chief inspector was evidently happy to have an excuse to set aside the job in hand, for he motioned him into a seat.

'Thorny, sorry you got waylaid by Jakes. I gather the trip to Derling was a waste of time; that man was never a serious suspect, but at least it's another name crossed off the list.' He glanced at the clock on the wall. 'You'll want to go. Big day tomorrow...'

'No sir, no need.' Deepbriar pulled a wry face. 'I've spent enough time on my speech, and I don't think I can do any better. There's something else I'd like to get started on, if it's all right with you. I was wondering if I could go to Cawster again. Somebody had a word with me while we were out at the quarry. That rumour Sergeant Parsons mentioned was always a long shot, but it turns out there was some truth in it.' He gave his superior a quick résumé of what he had heard from Riley.

'A member of this force suppressed information about an attempt to kidnap a child?' Stubbs looked incredulous. 'Even if it has no bearing on this case, or the death of Miriam Pitt, how could a thing like that

68

happen? This is a very serious business, Thorny.'

'I know, sir. And if you insist I'll tell you who was involved. But it was all a long time ago, and what's done can't be undone. The man who made the decision not to investigate is dead, and his subordinate isn't a policeman any longer.'

There was a short silence. 'So you're saying if we look for a scapegoat that's exactly what we'll get: some poor constable who was obeying orders.' Stubbs rubbed at his chin. 'It could be that you're a trifle biased, Constable, after what happened when you were just a rookie, but I'll go along with you for the moment. See what you can find out, and report back directly to me.'

'Thank you, sir.' Deepbriar turned to go.

'Oh, Thorny,' the chief inspector called him back. 'I hope everything goes well tomorrow. Have a good time. Just remember you're due here by eight on Sunday morning.'

Deepbriar grinned. 'You don't have to worry, sir, it'll be all champagne and fancy wine, not my sort of tipple. I doubt if I'll get a sniff of a pint.' On the way out to the bus stop, he remembered the auction; it would have been over hours ago. A feeling of foreboding came over him; a lowly country bobby didn't go buying a house, even a small one. He'd never really believed they could afford Mrs Twyford's cottage; they would have to take another look at the terraces on that Falbrough estate; the rents there were very reasonable. Mary would hate leaving Minecliff…

'Thorny!' The voice cut across his thoughts. Charles was waving to him from the other side of the road, standing by the Humber with Elaine's arm linked through his. Both of them were smiling, and Elaine gave him a thumbs up, her smile widening as she saw the shock on his face. She nodded vigorously.

He owned a house. Deepbriar, open-mouthed and stunned, stared across at his friends, both now openly laughing at him. His mind was turning somersaults. He hesitated on the kerb, seeing the Cawster bus approaching, but unable to recall why he'd intended to board it.

'Doesn't look as if you're safe to let out alone at the moment,' Charles said, taking hold of his elbow. 'Where's your bike?'

'I was… I haven't finished work yet.'

'It's nearly half past six, how much longer will you be?'

Coming to his senses, Deepbriar watched the bus pulling away. 'Actually, maybe I'm done after all. I just have to go and explain to the chief inspector.' Feeling as if he was walking on air, Thorny hurried back inside.

Deepbriar glanced at the organ loft as the

70

first notes rang out. He felt large and awkward standing beside his friend with the eyes of so many people upon them; the villagers had packed into the bride's side of the church, as all her family had died in the war. Deepbriar would far rather have been up there, in Bella Emerson's place, releasing beautiful, heart-stirring music from beneath his hands. His collar was tight, as were his new shoes. For the twentieth time he fingered the ring in his waistcoat pocket. Intent on leaving his military career behind, Charles had opted to get married in civvies; he too was fidgeting, as if he didn't feel quite at home in his new suit. Thorny looked round to see that he looked white as a sheet.

'You OK?' he whispered.

'Suppose she changes her mind,' Charles croaked back at him. 'She almost walked out on me once...'

'Don't be an idiot,' Thorny replied briskly, 'Listen.'

Beneath a quiet passage in the music, the sound of the old Humber's engine could be heard echoing against the high wall of the mill as it crossed the bridge, then purred away into silence before it drew up at the lichgate. A moment later Bella Emerson pulled out all the stops; there was a rush of triumphal music, which almost drowned the scraping of pews as the congregation rose to their feet, and the two men turned to steal a glance at the radiant bride as she processed up the aisle on Colonel Brightman's arm. Behind them came Mary Deepbriar, holding the bride's train and looking equally radiant; Elaine had designed the suit Mary had sewn for the occasion, and a stranger would never have guessed that she was expecting a child within a fortnight.

His nerves forgotten, Charles grinned at his friend. 'Doesn't seem long since the last time we stood here together,' he said quietly.

Deepbriar snorted. 'Wasn't much like this,' he whispered back. He and Mary had been married in this church, but it had been a ramshackle wartime wedding, and pure luck that Charles had been home on leave to act as best man.

The Reverend Robert Pusey discreetly cleared his throat, and they turned to face him, as Elaine took her place at Charles's side. Thorny was pleased to see that his friend's colour had improved a little; as he watched he saw the man take in a long slow breath, and knew that everything was going to be all right.

When the happy couple left the church they were greeted by three deafening cheers; it looked as if the whole of Minecliff had turned out to wish them well, and the clouds of confetti were so thick they covered the path like a layer of snow. While the colonel's old Humber carried the bride and groom back to the manor, five more cars followed with the guests who had been invited to the wedding breakfast. Having dispatched his duties thus far, Deepbriar was the last to climb into a vehicle, having to shoo some of his friends and neighbours away as they pretended to try joining him. The village troublemakers were rowdy with the excitement of the occasion; there would be two rounds of drinks for every man in the Speckled Goose, courtesy of the manor. Faced with making a speech, Deepbriar heartily wished he could join them.

He needn't have worried. Primed with a pint of beer, smuggled to him in the morning room by the colonel's housekeeper while the guests were finding their seats, Deepbriar's stories about his friend's childhood exploits raised several gusts of laughter, and the loudest of them rattled the windows, while his praise for the bride brought a hearty round of applause. He got through the toasts without one mistake, and when he sat down, blowing out his cheeks in relief, Mary reached across to pat his knee.

'See, I told you it would be all right,' she whispered.

Two hours later, with the newly-weds dispatched on their honeymoon, Colonel Brightman, with all due ceremony, informed Deepbriar that he was intending to make his next drive in the old Humber his last.

'I decided this was a fitting occasion,' he said. 'I shall drive you and Mrs Deepbriar home, and when Charles comes back from Scotland I shall turn this old girl over to him.' It took them a sedate five minutes to cover the short distance to the village. 'I don't see as well as I used to,' the colonel admitted as they climbed out of the car. 'Do you know, at our last shoot I only bagged one brace?'

Having thanked the old man and watched him drive away, Mary stood hesitating on the doorstep of the police house. She turned suddenly. 'Thorny, can we go to Stellings Lane? I still don't feel as if I've had the chance to introduce myself to the cottage, not properly; we were only there for a minute last night.'

'Why not?' Deepbriar delved into his pocket and pulled out a key. 'I'm not sure why I decided to carry this around all day. For luck, I think.' They walked slowly through the village, still dressed in their best, watched by children out playing in the last of the light.

The approaching darkness softened the shabbiness of their new home. Number four was badly in need of a coat of paint. 'I never really understood why Mrs Twyford moved here,' Thorny said. 'The Walnuts is a lovely old house.'

'It was too full of memories,' Mary said.

'Once her husband died she couldn't bear to stay in the place where they'd been so happy. This house belonged to him as well, of course, and it was empty, since the tenants had just moved out. Coming to Stellings Lane was the easiest thing to do. In time I think she might have got around to having the plumbing sorted out, and the front door painted. The garden came first with her, she loved being out of doors.'

Deepbriar put his arm around his wife and gave her a quick hug. 'Losing somebody you love takes a lot of getting over,' he said.

'Yes. But I'm not going to think about that. I've made up my mind to keep cheerful from now on. The baby deserves that, doesn't he? And look how lucky we are, having a child after all this time. Between the three of us we'll make this little house a happy home.'

Deepbriar smiled, hiding the fact that he couldn't share her mood. Somehow her words had reminded him of the job he would be undertaking the next day. Not all families were facing a happy future. Six years ago the parents of Miriam Pitt had gone through hell, and at any moment Mr and Mrs Smithers might be faced with the same horror. Tomorrow he would try to find ex-constable Toby Reeman, and maybe speak to some members of the notorious Craggs brood. It was possible that the death of at least one innocent little girl could have been prevented, or maybe even two, if somebody hadn't made a major mistake seven years ago. He hoped with all his heart that his suspicions were wrong, because if they weren't, he was about to become very unpopular.

Chapter Five

'This is is official police business,' Deepbriar said, holding up his identification. 'I'm looking for Mr Toby Reeman.' He was wearing the boots that had accompanied him during his last three years on the beat, and as the frowsty woman tried to shut the warped and peeling door in his face, he planted one foot firmly on the sill. 'I gather he lives here.'

The boarding-house keeper pursed her lips; wearing a grubby pinafore, and with her hair escaping untidily from the curlers half-hidden beneath a ragged head-square, she looked as run-down as her property. 'Not any more.'

'I'm sure he will have left a forwarding address.'

She shrugged. 'I've probably got it written down somewhere. Let me shut the door and I'll fetch it.'

'I've got a better idea.' Deepbriar put his weight against the door and stepped inside. 'You invite me in. Then you fetch it.'

Fifteen minutes' brisk walk took Deepbriar to the edge of Carrside, a crumbling warren of dreary terraced houses. They had been built in Victorian times of cheap bricks, long since stained black. The narrow road was pocked with holes, and most of the houses were sadly dilapidated, but the one he was looking for proved to be an exception; the tiny front garden was neat, and the woodwork had recently been painted. Deepbriar lifted the polished brass knocker.

A man in his fifties opened the door and looked at Deepbriar, the look of puzzlement being replaced swiftly by recognition. 'I know a copper when I see one. I've been half-expecting a visit. You weren't at Cawster during my time, but haven't we met?'

'It's possible. I'm DC Deepbriar.'

Reeman gave a slow nod. 'But you were in uniform back then. Derling, was it?'

'You're in the right direction,' Deepbriar replied. 'I was the village bobby in Minecliff. I've just made the move to Falbrough CID. Sorry to come bothering you on a Sunday. Sergeant Riley gave me your name.'

Reeman stood back. 'You'd best come in. I'm surprised you found me, I haven't kept in touch with any of the lads at the station.'

'You've moved about,' Deepbriar acknowledged, following him into the kitchen. 'I've seen a fair bit of the town, tracking you down. Decent little place you've got here; a bit better than the last one. The woman there did her best to close the door on me.'

Reeman grimaced. 'Yes, a proper tartar,

78

that one. It was all I could afford for a while, until I eventually found a decent job. It's not easy at my age. My wife died, two years after I left the force. She'd been ill a long time, and I couldn't leave her alone for more than a couple of hours, not during the last eighteen months, so I wasn't earning.'

'Things are looking up for you now, though?'

'Yes, this is comfortable enough. Decent landlord and a fair rent.' The man gestured at a chair and turned to pick up the kettle that was steaming gently on the hob. 'Tea?'

'That'd be nice, thanks. So, you were expecting somebody.' Deepbriar sat down at the kitchen table and watched ex-constable Reeman pour boiling water into the pot.

'Sort of. I'm assuming you're here about what happened a year before the little Pitt girl went missing.'

'I'm working from hearsay,' Deepbriar replied. 'I haven't got any details.'

'The similarity between the two cases should have been picked up. Trouble was, nothing was ever put in writing.' Reeman was quiet for a moment, then he ran a hand over his sparse head of hair. 'I'm glad you're here. After seven years I was beginning to wonder if it would ever be properly investigated; things can so easily be forgotten, and this business could give you a lead.'

'Perhaps you'd like to tell me exactly what

happened,' Deepbriar said. 'All I've got to go on is an old rumour and a couple of names.'

Bringing two mugs of tea to the table, Reeman settled himself comfortably opposite Deepbriar and took a sip of the hot, strong brew. 'Carrside was even rougher in those days than it is now,' he said. 'It was on my regular beat, but no copper went in there alone if he could avoid it. The sergeant knew what it was like; he'd do his best to send a second man, a new bloke or a probationer, anyone he could spare. It was the last Saturday in October, 1950. There was nobody free that day, because Cawster Rovers were playing at home. Luckily that made the area quieter than usual, so I wasn't expecting any trouble.'

Reeman's eyes were unfocused, his gaze fixed on some image in the past. 'I could hear a bit of a noise, and when I turned into Southcarr Road there was a bunch of women and kids on the pavement, milling around outside Ma Craggs's place. You not being local, you might not have heard of the Craggs clan. Villains, the whole lot of them. Petty theft, actual bodily harm, drunk and disorderly, burglary, running an illegal book – you name it. Anyway, when I got there, Ma turned on me. I'll spare your blushes and leave out all the four-letter words, but the gist of it was: what use were the effing coppers when little girls got set on by mucky-minded effing perverts, and when was I going to start earning my effing pay?'

'Nice neighbourhood,' Deepbriar said, as some comment seemed to be called for.

Reeman blew out a long breath. 'I thought for a minute I was going to find myself facing a mob. While Ma was shouting at me, one woman went and fetched a meat cleaver. She said if I wasn't going after him she'd sort the beggar out herself. Only she didn't say beggar.'

'So what did you do?'

'Don't ask me how, but I managed to calm things down. They told me that Ma Craggs's youngest, Annie, had been walking home with a friend when this man came and offered them a ride in his car, saying it was parked down by the canal. Luckily kids grow up fast in Carrside; they weren't silly enough to go with him. Annie took off. Her friend wasn't so quick and the man grabbed her. If Annie hadn't gone back and sunk her teeth into his hand, who knows how it might have ended, but as it was they both got away. Of course, by the time I'd been told all this I knew the man would be long gone, but I went to take a look. There was nothing to see at the spot where they said they'd met him, so I went on towards the canal. There aren't many places you can get a vehicle down there, and it would have taken him a while to turn a car round and get back to

81

the road. As I reached the towpath, I came face to face with Eddie, another of Ma Craggs's brats. He was pushing his bike. A proper bad boy, Eddie. He'd have been seventeen then, and he'd already been in court more than once.'

'There was an Edwin Craggs involved in an attack on a bank messenger last year,' Deepbriar remarked. 'Two men got ten years apiece, but Craggs had only been the lookout, so he was given three. A bit of a tough nut, by all accounts.'

'You're right there. Anyway, I stopped him, asked what he was up to, and he was all innocence, though it was hard to miss the fact that he'd been in a fight. He had the start of a black eye, and it looked as if he'd grazed his knuckles. I thought maybe Ma had sent him off as soon as Annie got back, and he'd caught up with this bloke and had it out with him. He didn't argue when I told him to walk back along the bank with me, though he was a bit uneasy when we reached Boulder Bridge. There was no car, only tyre tracks and a little splash of oil. But there was a spot of blood on the ground, and it was fresh.'

Reeman shrugged. 'It looked pretty conclusive, but I couldn't get a word out of Eddie. I'd no real evidence, since the man and the car had gone, so I told him to keep out of trouble, and let him go. That was it. I handed in a report, thinking CID would send somebody to interview the two girls at least, and maybe have words with Eddie. A week later, Ma Craggs stopped me in the street again, and started giving me another mouthful. She swore blind that nothing had been done, nobody had talked to Annie, or Eddie.'

'It was just forgotten?' Deepbriar was incredulous.

'Swept under the carpet.' Reeman nodded. 'I asked a mate who was in plain clothes, but he hadn't heard a thing, and when I asked him to do me a favour and look for my report, he couldn't find it. When Miriam Pitt vanished nearly a year later, I mentioned the incident to my sergeant again, but he said it was all nonsense, just kids larking about and having us on, and didn't I have more sense than to believe anything Ma Craggs told me? I was a bit miffed, so I went to have a word with young Annie. I was the only copper who'd spoken to her, and she hadn't changed her story, not a word, told it just the way her mother had relayed it to me.'

'You didn't leave it there?' Deepbriar hazarded; this man had been a decent copper.

Reeman sighed. 'I went over my sergeant's head and spoke to the inspector. All I got was a bollocking. A week later I was sent off to cover for a village bobby who'd gone sick. I took the hint. With only a couple of years to go before I retired, I wasn't going to risk rocking the boat.' He sat back in his chair, looking straight at Deepbriar across the table. 'I knew it was wrong, but I don't see what else I could have done. Still, it's stayed with me, all this time. You really think it's the same man, come back a third time?'

'For all our sakes I hope not,' Deepbriar said. 'It's a few years late, but I'd better have a word with Annie Craggs and her friend. Do you know the other girl's name?'

Reeman shook his head. 'No, sorry. I must have written it down at the time, but I can't remember. I saw her with Annie once or twice though. Pretty kid. Lovely fair hair.'

'Just like Miriam Pitt and Janey Smithers.' Deepbriar's voice was bleak.

Deepbriar trudged to the bus station after calling on Ma Craggs, feeling decidedly discouraged. The woman had been even worse than he'd expected from Reeman's description, and it had taken ten minutes of threats and cajoling to learn that Annie had run off to London, despite being barely eighteen. Deepbriar could hardly blame any youngster for wanting to escape from Ma Craggs, and when she told him she had no idea of her daughter's whereabouts he gave up any thoughts of interviewing the girl. The mere mention of Eddie had been enough to bring forth a flood of invective and abuse from his mother, and Deepbriar withdrew, completely forgetting that he hadn't asked the name of Annie's friend.

At least he knew where to find Eddie. He must visit the prison. As for the second girl, further investigations would have to wait until the next day; he would try tracing her through the school she and Annie had attended, and hope she hadn't run off to London too.

Back at the office, Sergeant Gough greeted Deepbriar with a grumble about being left alone in the office all morning, since all the other men on duty were still engaged in the hunt for Janey Smithers. Deepbriar couldn't help thinking that the investigation was going nowhere, and he was itching to push on with his own enquiries. If Stubbs had been in the office he might have asked his permission to visit Eddie Craggs, Sunday or no, but he wasn't ready to confide in Sergeant Gough; of all his new colleagues, Gough was the one he liked least. He didn't think their boss had much of an opinion of the man either.

Deepbriar found himself sitting behind a large heap of typing. Evidently the sergeant was suffering from a rheumatic condition which made such tasks difficult. It was particularly bad, the constable noted sourly, when there were no senior officers about. 'Oh, and the canteen shuts at three,' Gough said. 'Be a good lad and fetch me a cuppa in about half an hour.' With that he took himself off to have a chat with the desk sergeant.

The work progressed slowly. Deepbriar's thoughts drifted back seven years. If only Ma Craggs hadn't wasted time abusing Reeman the constable might have reached the canal before the child-molester left. The man would have been marked by Eddie's attack, and maybe by Annie's teeth – a factor which could have proved useful in identifying him. Shaking himself, the constable sighed; it was no good dwelling on might have beens.

The long boring afternoon drew to a close, with Deepbriar's eyes fluttering shut as he drooped over the typewriter. Gough had made his excuses and left, supposedly going to see a man who might have seen a car that might have been somewhere near the place where Janey's shoe was found. Given this news when he came in, Inspector Young looked sceptical. 'You might as well push off too,' he said. 'We're not even going round in circles. What we're doing is standing still and going nowhere, while this nasty bastard laughs at us.'

Deepbriar was tempted to tell him about his morning, but recalled that Stubbs had suggested they keep their suspicions to themselves for the present, so he merely shook his head in sympathy and took his leave.

Back home, he found Mary literally knee-deep in packing; she was standing in the bedroom with her hands clasped to her back, in obvious discomfort. After a moment's panic, thinking her pains had started, he scolded her for overdoing things, and told her to rest while he took over. They came close to arguing, and Deepbriar thumped out of the house to cycle to the other end of the village, where his sister-in-law lived. Being the eldest in a family of five, Agnes could always persuade her younger siblings to do as they were told. When she arrived she soon had Mary settled in an armchair with a cup of tea and a magazine. Agnes threw together a hasty meal before she helped Thorny to finish filling the packing-cases, a task Mary insisted was beyond a mere man to accomplish alone. By ten o'clock some semblance of order had been restored; Agnes went home, and Thorny followed his wife wearily up to bed.

'I'm sorry, love,' Mary said, unaccustomedly meek. 'I didn't mean – it's just the waiting, and getting so tired. I'm not used to being helpless.'

'I know,' Thorny assured her. 'I've been feeling pretty helpless today myself.'

'Do you want to tell me about it?'

He shook his head. 'All I need is a good night's sleep.'

Deepbriar didn't get his wish. The bad dreams which hadn't troubled him since his

87

convalescence in Bradsea came back with a vengeance, though now they featured a vengeful Ma Craggs, and an army of children with bright-yellow hair, and eyes shedding bloody tears. He'd found it worrying, for he'd seemed to make a full recovery from the serious concussion he'd suffered in the line of duty, but now began to wake several times a night, wide-eyed and sweating, and rose before the alarm clock sounded.

His head full of Annie Craggs and her friend, Deepbriar arrived at Falbrough station to find the place in uproar again. 'The Smithers case?' he asked hopefully, as Sergeant Parsons went by, thinking there might have been some development during the night.

The man shook his head. 'Another break-in. Cripps and Jones Packaging. But this time it looks as if they were disturbed. The watchman's been found dead.'

'Murdered?' Deepbriar was shocked. It was rare for burglars to turn violent and this particular villain had always seemed cool and professional, except in respect of the amount of stolen property he actually made off with. It seemed out of character for him to panic.

'Looks like it. Young Bartle was first on the scene. As soon as he telephoned me, I contacted Chief Inspector Stubbs; he's on his way in, and he said you and Constable Tidyman were to meet him there.' The sergeant gave him a knowing wink. 'Can't get by without his blue-eyed boy, can he? The man who finally brought Clive Beenham to justice.'

Deepbriar grunted, saved from any need to reply to this jibe by the arrival of Constable Tidyman.

The body of Cripps & Jones's night watchman lay in a corridor, a few yards from the front entrance of the vast building, and quite close to the little cubbyhole where the man was provided with a chair, a tap and a gas ring, to while away the time when he wasn't walking his rounds. The corpse was slumped uncomfortably between wall and floor, with the head propped up against a fire extinguisher. Deepbriar thought the dead man's sightless gaze had something of reproach about it.

Detective Chief Inspector Stubbs nodded at Deepbriar and Tidyman. 'Nasty dent in the back of his head. Bit of a surprise though,' he added. 'This villain's been so careful to get in and out without any fuss, not even making a mess when he's turning the place over. What did he want to go hitting an old man for?'

'Because he was seen?' Tidyman ventured. 'He wouldn't want to be identified.'

Stubbs shook his head. 'But the cases weren't exactly serious. If they were taken to court, at the most he'd have been given a couple of years. Why risk going to the gallows?'

'He must have panicked,' Tidyman said.

'Maybe. But why come along here at all?' Deepbriar said, looking at the blank grey walls of the long corridor, furnished only with the fire extinguisher and an elderly metal cabinet, which proved to be empty. 'The offices are over the other side; there's nothing here to steal, unless he was after a few cardboard boxes. Our villain usually seems to know where he's going. Where did he break in this time?'

'That's what I want you to find out. I sent young Bartle to have a quick look, but he's not reported back. The petty cash has gone, as usual, and the cashier tells me his desk has been searched, though how he can tell I'm blowed if I know; it looks perfectly neat and tidy to me, just like all the other jobs.'

'Where am I likely to find Constable Bartle, sir?' Deepbriar asked. 'It might be worth me asking what he's already checked. No point going over the same ground twice.'

'I sent him to search out the back.' Stubbs grimaced. 'Tell the truth, the youngster looked a bit green around the gills, I didn't want him throwing up over the body.'

Concerned, Deepbriar went looking for his young friend and protégé, and found him studying a few shards of glass that lay among the weeds under a broken window.

90

'Morning, Thorny.' Harry Bartle looked pale, but in no danger of being sick. 'It looks as if this bloke is pretty nifty on his feet. He must have balanced on the dustbin, heaved himself up, broken the window somehow and swung himself inside.'

'Looks that way,' Deepbriar agreed. 'You all right? The chief said you felt poorly.'

The young man grimaced. 'I'm just starved. I worked a double shift yesterday, and I didn't have time for a meal. I've had nothing since breakfast yesterday, except a cup of tea. The canteen staff don't arrive in there for another hour yet so I can't beg for a bite to eat.'

'Why didn't you tell the Chief Inspector?'

'It makes me look a proper idiot,' Harry replied.

'You're more of an idiot to do nothing about it,' Deepbriar told him. 'Hang on.' He went to the car he and Tidyman had arrived in and raided the glove box; as he hoped, there was the crumpled paper bag. Only half a dozen sweets remained, but they would do.

'Thanks,' Harry said, round a surreptitious mouthful.

'Just don't let Stubbs catch you eating sweets on duty,' Deepbriar said. 'Right. They got into the building here, but how about the perimeter fence?'

'Beyond that patch of weeds,' Harry

91

replied indistinctly. 'It backs on to the canal, so it would be pretty quiet at night. I found a few smears in the mud, but nothing useful.'

With Harry fortified by three barley sugars, they went back to report their findings to the chief inspector. The old man's body had been removed, and Tidyman was on his hands and knees, searching the cubbyhole where the watchman had spent most of his time.

Sergeant Jakes had arrived, and stood at the chief inspector's side as Deepbriar explained what he and Harry Bartle had found.

'All right,' Stubbs said. 'We've got nowhere with any of the other cases, and it's not likely we'll find anything useful in here. There's a housing estate on that side of the site, and the main road forms a barrier to the north. I want house to house. We're looking for anybody who was out late yesterday evening, or during the night: shift workers, mothers who were up with sick kids. You never know, they might have seen something.'

'What about the canal, sir?' Sergeant Jakes asked.

'Yes, there's often a boat or two at the moorings further downstream. They'll have moved on by now. Deepbriar, you'd better cover that. Get down to the locks first, or they'll be halfway to Birmingham before you know it. I'll get on to the super and tell him we need extra manpower, though lord knows where we'll find it, with the Smithers case taking up so much time. You can make a start on house to house, Sergeant, and I'll send Tidyman out once he's finished here.'

'Yes sir. Any idea what time we're interested in?'

'The old man had apparently been dead quite a while; at the very latest, he died at midnight, so we'll say up to one o'clock this morning. Right, get to it.'

Deepbriar half-opened his mouth, wanting to tell his boss about the results of his investigation the day before, but with a resigned shrug he turned away. For the moment this new case must come first. Everyone knew that the first day of a murder enquiry was the most important; miss some clue now, and it could be disastrous.

Chapter Six

Monday oozed seamlessly into Tuesday and Deepbriar was barely aware that he had eaten and slept at some time in between. He trudged the streets of Falbrough, half-awake, conducting house-to-house enquiries around the Cripps & Jones site. Other officers were busy interviewing the men and women who worked there, while Chief Inspector Stubbs and Constable Tidyman were calling on all the known local villains, as well as the local snouts, those much despised characters who hung around the criminal fraternity, seeking out tit-bits of information which might be worth the price of a few pints.

Reaching home comparatively early on Tuesday night, at around seven, Deepbriar spent four hours helping Mary to sort out more of their belongings, and carrying packing cases from the police house to Stellings Lane. He retired wearily to bed, but terrible dreams continued to disturb the constable's sleep; he couldn't get the images of Janey Smithers and Miriam Pitt out of his head. On the pretext that his wife would be more comfortable with extra room to accommodate her ever expanding waistline, he spent most of the night on the settee downstairs, waking with an aching head and eyes full of grit.

With Chief Inspector Stubbs now involved with the new case, Inspector Young had been given temporary charge of the Janey Smithers investigation, helped by Sergeant Jakes and two men from Cawster. Jakes was at his desk when Deepbriar walked into the office. The sergeant yawned into his hand. There was no need to ask if they were making progress, his slumped body told its own tale. 'We're not going to get this evil beggar, Thorny,' he said resignedly, 'not without a flipping miracle. There's no way we're going to find that kid alive. It's only been ten days, but the case is stone cold. No leads, not a sniff of a suspect.'

Deepbriar opened his mouth, thinking that now, if ever, was the time to share what he'd learnt from Reeman, but at that instant Chief Inspector Stubbs came in. The constable snapped his jaw shut so suddenly that it hurt.

'Could you spare me a moment, sir?'

Ushered into his superior's office, Deepbriar brought him up to date, relating what he'd learnt from ex-constable Reeman and Ma Craggs. 'I can't see why the CID in Cawster didn't follow it up, sir. Nobody even spoke to Annie Craggs and the other girl.'

95

'I don't know, Thorny,' Stubbs said, rubbing his chin. 'There must have been a reason. The Craggs family are notoriously unreliable; telling lies is second nature to people like that. And with kids, well, you never know what goes on in their heads.'

'But it looks as if Eddie Craggs found a man down by the canal, and attacked him,' Deepbriar persisted. 'If the girls invented the whole thing, and he beat up an innocent man, surely his victim would have reported him to the police?'

Stubbs thought about it and nodded reluctantly. 'It's a good point. Look, as soon as things ease off, you can talk to Eddie Craggs, and see if you can locate the girl. But bear in mind, this was only ever a shot in the dark; don't set too much store by what you find. Even if things happened the way the girls said, it doesn't necessarily make the man who accosted them a killer.'

It was true, Deepbriar reflected, squeezing his aching eyes shut for a moment before he returned to his desk. For the tenth time that week he wondered if he'd been a fool to leave Minecliff; he could have stayed put until retirement. After lunch, fighting off sleep, Deepbriar was jolted to wakefulness by the sound of the chief inspector's voice. 'I can't be in two places at once, sir.' Stubbs sounded unusually irritable, and Deepbriar glanced surreptitiously at the two men

96

coming in through the door, not surprised to see that Stubbs was accompanied by Chief Superintendent Murray.

'Send somebody else to talk to Wilson then,' Murray barked. 'We can't afford to waste any more time. An abduction and a murder, both inside a fortnight, and the lord knows you got nowhere with the first case.' The door slammed shut as the man stormed out, and Stubbs stood for a moment, staring after him. Then he seemed to give himself a shake and he looked around the room. 'Thorny, you look as if you could do with some fresh air. Our boss seems to think Digger Wilson might know something. He's moved out of town, the other side of Cawster somewhere. See if you can track him down. Constable Tidyman can drive you.'

Deepbriar's eyebrows shot up. 'Digger Wilson? He must be seventy if he's a day.'

'Seventy-five more like. Just do it, Constable.' Stubbs went into his office, closing the door with exaggerated care.

Sharing Stubbs's belief that it was a waste of time, Deepbriar made the most of his excursion into the countryside with young Constable Tidyman, who was a much less flamboyant driver than Sergeant Jakes. It took them three hours to find Wilson, who had been a valued police informer many years ago. He had, he told them proudly, lived over eighty years, but he had been retired for nearly ten of them, and he had no idea who might be breaking into factories in Falbrough.

'Murder?' Wilson shook his head when they told him what had happened at Cripps & Jones. 'Don't sound likely, does it, not when all he's after is a bit of cash? If I knew owt I'd tell you, free and gratis, seeing I'm not working any more, but the villains from my time are mostly dead and gone.'

Deepbriar looked at his watch as they returned to the car; it would be the end of their shift by the time they got back to the station, and they would have to pass through Cawster on the way. If they were quick, and Tidyman agreed to drop him off, he might have time to visit King Edward School, once attended by Annie Craggs.

Puffing a little, Deepbriar almost ran up the hill from the bus station. Teachers didn't keep the same hours as their pupils, but it was late, thanks to Tidyman getting lost in a maze of country lanes, and as he reached the school gates he heard the clock in a nearby church strike six.

The front door was closed, but there were lights on inside the school. Deepbriar rapped his knuckles on the varnished wood and waited hopefully. Nobody came. He knocked harder the second time, and after some delay a grey-haired woman, thin-faced and severe of manner, opened the door and stared discouragingly at him.

'Whatever it is you want, you're too late,' she said. 'The school will reopen at 8.30 tomorrow morning.'

Deepbriar introduced himself, still a little breathless. 'I apologize for coming at this hour,' he said, 'but I need some information about a former pupil. She may have information that is relevant to the Janey Smithers case.'

Her expression didn't soften; he rather doubted if it could, but her voice was a little less abrupt when she spoke again. 'I'm the deputy headmistress, Miss Chambers. I'm afraid it's unlikely I'll be able to assist you.' However, she opened the door wider and ushered him inside. 'Come into my office for a moment. If I can't answer your questions, I can at least tell you who you'll need to see, and when it would be best to return.'

Perched on a hard chair, Deepbriar looked at the formidable woman across a wide oak desk, and did his best to dismiss memories of his own schooldays. 'Were you teaching at this school seven years ago, Miss Chambers?' he asked.

'I was,' she said, 'but I have to warn you that I don't know every child by name. We have over one hundred pupils in each year. Since we use the streaming system, and I teach mathematics at the highest level, there are many children who never attend my classes.'

'But a girl who was notorious for other reasons, even if she wasn't clever at mathematics, perhaps she would leave an impression?'

She gave a grave nod. 'That does happen. Of whom are you speaking?'

'A girl by the name of Annie Craggs. Or, to be more exact, her friend. At least, they were friends some six or seven years ago. All I know about this other girl is that she was a pretty child, with blond hair, and that she probably lived near Carrside, though not actually on the estate.'

Miss Chambers nodded again. 'That will be June,' she replied. 'June Day.' She was far too well-mannered to grimace, but her face showed her distaste. 'Some parents don't seem to think before choosing a name for their child. Fortunately she is, as you say, a pretty girl, and I've seen no sign that she suffers excessively from teasing.'

'The way you speak about her, it sounds as if she's still here.' Deepbriar said.

'June is in the sixth form, and one of our brightest hopes.' There was pride in the austere voice now. 'It is likely she'll win a scholarship to Cambridge University, a first for a girl from this school.'

'Very commendable,' Deepbriar replied,

seeing that a response was called for. 'But are you sure she's the right girl? She sounds an unlikely friend for one of the Craggs clan.'

'She and Annie were very close for a while. I confess the liaison worried me, but the friendship faded over time, when Annie gravitated towards others of her own kind. I do not believe in categorizing children on account of their class, Constable, but friendships are always more successful when the parties share a degree of intellectual ability. That is one advantage of streaming, it places those of similar capabilities together. Annie was not unintelligent, you understand, but despite all our efforts we could never persuade her to apply herself. We still have two of her younger siblings here, and are faring no better with either of them.'

'It must be difficult,' Deepbriar murmured. This was definitely not a woman to cross, and he felt almost sorry for the dreadful Ma's children, who failed to come up to Miss Chambers' standards. 'I wonder if you could let me have June Day's address?'

'I'm afraid I can't.' She quelled the beginnings of his protest with a look. 'The secretary, Mrs Morrison, keeps all the student records locked in her filing cabinet, and I'm afraid I don't have a key. If you care to return tomorrow morning, any time after

8.30...?' She rose from her chair, to indicate that the interview was over.

As Miss Chambers held the front door open she suddenly checked. 'I don't know if this is relevant to your investigation, Constable, but June was once involved with another member of the Craggs family, Edwin. It was a most regrettable association; he was a good deal older than she. Fortunately, the entanglement ended when he was sent to prison.'

Heavy rain began to fall as Deepbriar made his way back down the hill towards the bus stop. It was a disappointment to have got no further in his search, but at least he had a name, and tomorrow he would learn the address. Did June's involvement with Eddie have any bearing on the events down by the canal? She'd been a child then, surely too young to attract the attention of a youth who was six or seven years her senior.

The bus shelter was already overflowing with passengers, and Deepbriar found what protection he could from the rain by standing under a nearby tree. Evidently there had been no buses along for half an hour. When one arrived it was already full, and the conductor smilingly waved the newcomers aboard, pushing those already standing into closer contact, to make room for them. 'Have your fares ready if you please,' he called, laughing, 'and mind your backs. I'm

102

only coming through once.'

Deepbriar scowled, steaming and swaying as he endured an unpleasant version of sardines, jammed against a man who smelt of wet dog. Fortunately, by the time they were halfway to Minecliff, most of the passengers had alighted, and Deepbriar sank gratefully into a seat. He was sound asleep when the bus pulled up outside the Speckled Goose, and the conductor gave his shoulder a brisk shake.

'Home, Constable,' he said, still irrepressibly cheerful. 'Mind the step.'

Deepbriar stumbled over the road, dazed and slightly dizzy. He was reminded of the time he'd been concussed; his eyes seemed reluctant to focus, and it was all he could do not to simply sink down where he stood and fall asleep. Mary took one look at him and ordered him straight upstairs. 'I'll bring your meal up,' she said, 'and no argument. Get those wet things off and into bed. You'll be no sort of a father to Deepbriar junior if you're sick with pneumonia.'

It was a measure of his exhaustion that he didn't attempt to argue. When he woke next morning, jolted into consciousness by the discordant ring of the alarm clock, he had little recollection of having eaten his tea, but an empty plate lying on the floor suggested that he must have had a meal.

'How do you feel?' Mary asked, as he

joined her in the kitchen a few minutes later. 'You looked like death last night.'

'Better,' Deepbriar replied, giving her a quick hug, 'thanks love. I don't have time for breakfast though, I left my bike at work, so I have to catch the bus.' He stared around the room, strangely bare now that most of the packing was done. 'Are we all ready?'

'I think so. You're sure you'll be back here by two?'

'At the very latest. Look, don't go over-doing things. If there's still packing–'

'I've got half the WI calling in,' Mary assured him placidly, 'and I doubt if they'll allow me out of my chair all morning.' She put a slice of buttered toast in his hand. 'Go on, you can eat that on your way to the door.'

Upon arriving at his desk Deepbriar found that all the files regarding the previous factory break-ins had been stacked on his desk. 'Are these here for me?' he asked. Constable Tidyman nodded towards Stubbs's office. 'The boss is getting desperate now that we're looking for a murderer. He wants you to see if there's anything we've missed.' He grinned, lowering his voice. 'I think you're supposed to do the Sherlock Holmes thing, you know. Tell him the colour of the beggar's hair, how tall he is, and whether he smokes ciggies or a pipe.'

Sergeant Jakes sniggered. Deepbriar

grunted, ignoring the younger men's mirth, and pulled the first folder towards him. He'd hardly begun reading when the office door was flung open, and Sergeant Parsons rushed in, heading straight for the chief inspector's room. At the very moment when he lifted his hand to rap at the door, Stubbs came out, and it was only by a bit of smart footwork that the sergeant avoided a major collision, though he couldn't hang on to the file he'd been holding, which skidded across the floor and landed under Jakes's desk.

'Sorry sir,' he said breathlessly, pulling his tunic straight as Jakes recovered the file, mouth quirking as he tried not to laugh, and rose to hand the folder to Stubbs.

'You said you wanted the post mortem report on the old man at Cripps and Jones as soon as it arrived,' Parsons said, recovering his composure.

The chief inspector drew out two sheets of paper and scanned them quickly. 'Do me a favour, Sergeant Parsons,' he said, his expression grim. 'Recall the men investigating the murder at Cripps and Jones. It seems there wasn't one. The old man died of natural causes. No suggestion of foul play. He had a heart attack. The blow to the head was delivered by the wall when he fell; he had an unnaturally thin skull, evidently. As far as they can say, there's no evidence that the heart attack was brought on by a sudden scare, and anyway, he died quite soon after the factory closed for the day, so he was probably dead several hours before the place was robbed.'

'Why did it take them so long to work that out, sir?' Jakes demanded, once Parsons had gone. 'The post mortem was held yesterday, wasn't it?'

'We were treating it as a suspicious death, so when the chap who examined the body failed to find any evidence of foul play, he asked for a second opinion. This is it. No murder.'

'Chief Inspector?' the young uniformed constable who had been manning the main desk with Sergeant Parsons had come in. His face was pale, his expression intense. The room fell suddenly silent. 'Inspector Young just telephoned. They've found a little girl's body, and it matches the description of Janey Smithers. He says please will you meet him at Everscombe Farm.'

Stubbs straightened, his face taut. 'We've spent two days chasing a murderer who doesn't exist, when we should have been looking for this damned child-killer. Tidyman, I'll need a driver. Deepbriar, forget the break-ins. I'm getting desperate enough to try anything. Share what you've found out about that rumour with Sergeant Jakes; the pair of you can follow up whatever leads you

106

have. You've got carte blanche, I'll back you in any investigation you care to make, and if anybody doesn't like it you can refer them to me.'

Chapter Seven

Keeping the tale as brief as possible, Deepbriar told Jakes about the incident involving Annie Craggs, and then explained that he now knew the name of her friend, who still lived in Cawster, although he didn't yet have her address. 'She'll be at school by now,' he finished. 'It would save time if we went and spoke to her there.'

'And we need to talk to Eddie,' Jakes said, animated now that they had a lead, even if it was a tenuous one. 'Right, Thorny, school first, then the prison. I met Craggs once, he's a hard nut. Talking of nuts, if he doesn't cooperate we could try hammering his head against the wall. That's what my old boss at Belston would have done.'

'I don't reckon that'll be necessary,' the constable replied, reflecting dismally that he had to endure hours in a car with Jakes again. 'Eddie has a weak spot.'

June Day was very pretty; her bright hair seemed to light up the room when Miss Chambers brought her into her office. The girl looked serious but not concerned at being introduced to two CID officers, evidently she had no guilty secrets to hide.

'I believe I should remain,' Miss Chambers said.

Sergeant Jakes nodded. 'You will appreciate that what we say here is not to be repeated,' he said, 'and I'd be obliged if you don't interrupt.' He sat in the plush visitor's chair, brought forward from its place in a corner. Deepbriar hadn't noticed it the night before, and was wryly amused that, as a mere detective constable, he hadn't merited its use.

Deepbriar remained standing, notebook in hand. During their journey to the school he had given the sergeant a full briefing, though his concentration hadn't been helped by the expectation of being involved in a car smash at any minute.

Quickly and efficiently, Jakes confirmed that June had been Annie Craggs's close friend during their first year at secondary school, and she perfectly recalled the day when the two of them had been accosted in the park.

'I yelled when he took hold of me,' June said, 'and Annie came back.' She glanced at Miss Chambers, half defensive, half defiant. 'Annie was a good friend. She bit the man on the hand, and made him let go. I still wouldn't have escaped if she hadn't grabbed my arm and pulled me along. I'd just sort of frozen, and anyway, I'm no good at running.'

109

'Did he follow you?'

She nodded. 'I was terrified. My mum had told me never to go off with strangers, but nothing like that had ever happened before, not to anybody we knew; even Annie was fairly innocent back then.' She flushed. 'She changed though. It was when she started going around with boys, and talking about the things they said and did, that I stopped seeing her.'

'By the age of thirteen the silly girl was associating with boys from Carrside Technical College,' Miss Chambers said disapprovingly.

Jakes turned to remind her that she was supposed to keep quiet, but the schoolmistress met his look and with a slight shrug he returned his attention to June. 'Were you ever interviewed by the police about this incident?' he asked.

June shifted in her seat as if it had become suddenly too hard. 'No,' she said. 'Annie told me her mum had talked to a policeman about it.'

'What about your parents? Surely they were concerned about what had happened?'

The reason for the girl's discomfort revealed itself. 'I never told them,' she said. 'They didn't like me being friends with Annie, I wasn't even supposed to walk home with her. My dad works at the bank, he was always going on about his position, and how

110

I was letting him down by hanging around the Carrside estate.'

Jakes glanced across at Deepbriar. This had probably been why the incident hadn't been investigated; a complaint by June's father wouldn't have been ignored.

'So, how did you get away?' Jakes queried.

For the first time, June hesitated. 'Annie started shouting.'

'If she had enough breath left to shout, you'd stopped running, is that right?'

'We reached the park gates and looked back, and he'd gone,' she said, the reply coming more readily this time, although Deepbriar noticed that she hadn't exactly answered Jakes's question. 'A bus came along, and all I wanted to do was get back home. I had some of my pocket money, enough to pay the fare for both of us, but Annie wouldn't come. We started arguing, and the conductor got cross, so in the end I went on my own.'

'Can you describe the man who attacked you?' Jakes asked. 'Would you recognize him if you saw him again?'

'I don't think so. It was a long time ago – I used to have nightmares,' she added, 'but even in my dreams I never saw his face properly. He was wearing a hat, pulled down low, and a long coat.'

'Do you recall what sort of hat?' Jakes lifted the rather jaunty hat that he held on

111

his knee. 'Anything like this? Or more like the constable's trilby?'

'It had a big brim. And it was black, or very dark brown.' Somewhere a bell rang and the girl looked at Miss Chambers. 'I should be at maths.'

'As should I,' the woman said. 'Have you finished, Sergeant?'

As Jakes nodded, looking as if he was about to rise to his feet, Deepbriar spoke. 'If I might ask something?' he put in diffidently. 'Are you still in touch with Annie Craggs, June?'

'No. We've not been friends for years. I heard she'd gone to London.'

'Was it Eddie who told you that?'

June stared at her feet. 'Yes,' she said, the word barely audible.

'You and Eddie walk out together.' Deepbriar said.

She shook her head, her gaze still downcast. 'Not any more, not after what he did.'

'You mean when he got in trouble with the law. But before that, it must have been flattering, him being a lot older than you. Seventeen, wasn't he, that day in the park? He must have seemed very grown up.' Deepbriar felt Jakes's eyes turn on him, but he kept watching June, trying to read her thoughts. It was a pure guess of course, but he had a feeling she had something else to tell them. 'Did you think he was a bit of a hero?'

Her head jerked up, and she stared at the constable in surprise. 'Have you been talking to Eddie? I never thought he'd tell anyone....'

'Perhaps you'd better tell us the whole story,' Jakes prompted.

Again, June seemed to find the lino under her feet of great interest. 'We were running across the park, and the man was right behind us. I couldn't keep up with Annie, and he would have caught me if Eddie hadn't come along. Eddie threw down his bike and started swearing at the man and punching him. I didn't see it all. I felt dizzy, so I leant against a tree and put my head down. When I looked up Eddie was chasing the man across the football pitch. I don't know what happened then. Annie and I went to the bus stop, like I said.'

'Didn't you ever ask Eddie how it ended? Later, perhaps, when the two of you were walking out together?'

'We only went to the pictures a few times,' June replied, looking worriedly at her teacher. 'I did try to talk about it once, but he said he'd forgotten, and that I should too.'

Miss Chambers had risen to her feet. 'If this is to go on any longer, I shall have to make provision for my class,' she said sternly.

'That's all right, thank you, Miss Chambers. I believe we've finished,' Sergeant Jakes said, looking at Deepbriar.

The constable nodded. 'I can't think of anything else,' he said.

Jakes got up and put the visitor's chair back by the wall. He smiled at the girl. 'Thank you for answering all our questions. You've been a great help.'

'You won't tell my mum and dad, will you?' For the first time the girl looked younger than her eighteen years.

'Not unless we have to,' Sergeant Jakes assured her. 'We'll see. It may depend on whether Eddie decides to cooperate.'

'Perhaps you should think about telling them yourself,' Deepbriar suggested gently. He opened the door and let June walk out before him. 'It was a long time ago and you were very young. I don't think they'll blame you for keeping quiet about it, not now you've given up your friendship with the Craggs family.'

The girl nodded, but her expression was suddenly bleak.

'I suppose everyone tells you what a bad lot Eddie is?' Deepbriar said softly.

She nodded again. 'He's not as bad as they say,' she whispered fiercely, glancing back at the office, where Jakes was thanking Miss Chambers. 'He didn't want to get involved in that robbery, but they made him.'

'He could have offered to help the police when they caught him,' Deepbriar said.

'They'd have killed him. Anyway, nobody

114

will ever believe he'd turned over a new leaf. Once you give a dog a bad name, that's the end of it.' She sounded desolate. 'Belonging to a family like that, what hope has he got?'

Miss Chambers caught up with them then, and with a cluck of her tongue she ushered June away. The girl gave Deepbriar a last despairing glance. Obviously giving up Eddie Craggs hadn't been as easy for June as everyone assumed.

Jakes was sceptical when Deepbriar reported what June had said about Eddie's wish to reform. 'He did his national service, and that didn't straighten him out,' he said.

'He was younger then. And he hadn't got a girl like June waiting for him.' Deepbriar made a grab for the strap above the door as they swerved wildly round a corner. 'She's still got a soft spot for him, and I'd be surprised if he doesn't have a weakness for her, too.'

'Well, if he really wants to turn over a new leaf, he can start by helping us with our enquiries,' Jakes said. 'I'm not messing about with a toerag like Craggs, Thorny. We have to make him talk. When we get in there I'd like you to stand behind him and make him feel uncomfortable. I'm not exactly intimidating, but you've got the size for it.'

'I don't go in for beating people up,' Deepbriar protested. He had been the victim of a sadistic schoolmaster in his childhood, and

115

he took no pleasure in violence.

'It's all right, I'm not asking you to hit him, just look as if you might.'

With reluctance Deepbriar agreed. 'What if it doesn't work?'

'I doubt if it will, but that's where we get clever. I'll find some reason to leave the room, and you try turning into the kindly father figure. See if you're right about him and June Day; tell him that two other pretty little kids like her have been taken away and murdered, and hope he develops a conscience.'

Jakes accelerated to overtake a car. 'That reminds me,' he said, grinning, 'the chief is still keen on you learning to drive. We'll have to arrange some more lessons. Maybe you could take over a bit on the way home, if this doesn't take too long?'

'I don't think there's time,' Deepbriar said. 'I'm sorry, but I've got the afternoon off.'

'How did you wangle that? You already had a whole day last Saturday.'

'We're moving house. I can't leave Mary to do it all on her own. The baby's due any time now.'

'Of course,' Jakes half-laughed. 'You're going to be a real father.'

Deepbriar nodded and lapsed into silence, reflecting gloomily that the baby would be coming into a state of chaos, with most of their possessions in boxes. Even worse, it

116

would be living in a house with no bathroom. He didn't know when he'd have time to get in touch with a builder.

With a protesting shriek from the tyres, Jakes brought the car to a halt outside the prison gates, and leant out to speak to the guard who came to peer in at the window.

The interview with Eddie Craggs didn't start well. The prisoner met all Jakes's threats and attempts at persuasion with the same blank stare, and never said a word. Looking as if he was on the verge of losing his temper, the sergeant rose to his feet. 'I want answers, Craggs, and if you won't give them willingly, then we'll try the hard way.' He stormed out, barking 'I'll be ten minutes,' to the constable.

Deepbriar shifted his feet. He had a feeling that Craggs would win any sort of waiting game, so after a few moments of silence, he walked across the room and sat down in the chair Jakes had vacated, pushing aside the file the sergeant had left on the table.

'Might as well take the weight off,' he said. 'Don't reckon you took to the sergeant much.'

Craggs muttered something under his breath. It was the first sound he'd made since he entered the room, so the constable took this as an encouraging sign. 'You what?' he prompted.

'Reminded me of my bloody drill sergeant,' Craggs said.

'Funny, I can't picture him in uniform, even as a copper. I never knew him before he joined CID. We called on June Day,' Deepbriar added conversationally. 'She's a pretty girl.'

The young man had lapsed back into silence, but something in his eyes changed. Deepbriar pressed on. 'I got the impression June doesn't think you're as black as you're painted. She told me you didn't want any part of that attack on the bank messenger.'

Craggs shifted his gaze and met Deepbriar's eyes for the first time. 'So what?' he said sullenly. 'Makes no difference, does it? Not now I'm stuck in here.'

'I'd have thought it might make a difference, having a lovely girl like that waiting for you. If you behave yourself, you could get parole in less than a year.'

'Still be long enough. She'll have gone off to mix with all them posh types. She reckons she's going to be a teacher or something. A girl like June, she'll meet some toff and forget I ever existed.' Craggs shrugged, slumping in his chair again, eyes focused on the floor. 'When I got dragged in on that job, she told me she never wanted to see me again.'

'Her parents probably put a lot of pressure on her. And I can't say I blame them. June hasn't given up on you, though. She'll soon be old enough to make up her own mind.'

Craggs said nothing, and for a moment

Deepbriar thought he was going to get no further. Perhaps it had been a mistake trying to win the young man's confidence; according to police records he was a hardened offender.

The silence stretched for over a minute.

'What did June say about me then?' Craggs growled suddenly.

Deepbriar pondered for a moment before he answered, looking for the right way to tackle this request. 'She said you were the dog that had been given a bad name. And that with a family like yours, you never had much of a chance.'

'Ain't that a fact,' Craggs drawled, almost amused. 'You ever meet my dad?'

Deepbriar shook his head. 'Look,' he said, 'if you really want to make something of your life when you get out, there are people who can help.'

'Huh. I've heard about all these do-gooders. They'd get me a nice steady job, sweeping floors or pushing barrows. June'd be really impressed.'

'There's only one person who can really change your life, Eddie,' Deepbriar said, 'and that's you. I thought you should know how June feels, and I've told you.'

'Yeah, thanks.' It was grudging, but Deepbriar thought the sentiment was genuine. It was time to see if he could get anything in return.

'Eddie, will you tell me about that day in the park? I reckon you caught up with the man who tried to molest June and your sister, all those years ago. And you gave him a hiding. Telling the truth won't get you into any more trouble, I promise.'

The mulish expression he'd worn when Jakes tried to question him came back on Eddie Craggs's face. Deepbriar sighed, but persevered. Although Eddie gave no sign that he was listening, the constable related what they knew about Janey Smithers's abduction. When this brought no response he went over the case of Miriam Pitt, which had been so similar, and just as impossible to crack.

'Fact is, Eddie, there's a chance that the man you chased that day could be a murderer. And you might be able to give us a lead. You got close to him, didn't you? Very close. And maybe you saw the car he'd left hidden by the canal. Some evil lowlife molested those two little girls, then killed them, Eddie. That could have been Annie and June.'

Eddie shook his head. 'He'd never have got hold of Annie, she's tough. She'd have scratched his eyes out.'

'But not June. Suppose Annie hadn't been there to fight the man off and pull her away? Or suppose you hadn't come along when you did?'

Craggs balled his fists. 'I don't like blokes who muck about with little kids.'

'Nobody does.' Deepbriar glanced at the door, hoping the sergeant wouldn't come back; at last he was getting somewhere. 'Just between you and me, Eddie, what happened?'

Chapter Eight

'It's quite a detailed description,' Deepbriar said, flipping open his notebook. 'I know it's a long shot, but if the same man took Miriam and Janey, then with Eddie's help we might be able to identify him.' He sighed. 'Not that it would be enough to bring any charges with relation to Janey or Miriam, it's all so circumstantial.'

'Read out what Craggs told you,' Jakes ordered. They were in the car, heading away from the prison. 'I've spent hours looking at the files of likely suspects, and there are some I've not been able to trace. Maybe this is one of them.'

'Right. Average height, five foot six or seven, no more. Thickset. Eddie reckoned the bloke was probably nearly twice his weight. Slightly protruding ears. His skin was very pale, as if it didn't get any sun–'

'Perhaps he'd been inside. There's nothing like a spell in prison to take the colour out of a man's cheeks,' Jakes put in.

Deepbriar ignored the interruption. 'His hair was black, and smoothed flat across his head.'

'June said he was wearing a hat,' Jakes said.

'Eddie knocked it off during the fight, and kicked it into the long grass.' Deepbriar shook his head in frustration. 'If only somebody had followed this up at the time, that hat might have been found. Right, what else was there? Eddie wasn't too sure about the man's age. Thirtyish? As for his clothes, he was wearing a long overcoat, charcoal grey, and it looked expensive, not like anything you'd see around Carrside.'

'The description doesn't ring any bells, but you're right, it's pretty clear,' Jakes said.

'That's not all. He told me something interesting about the car too. It was a big old Daimler saloon.'

Jakes gave a low whistle. 'That shouldn't be so hard to trace. This is brilliant, Thorny, you did a good job getting him to talk.'

Deepbriar hardly heard the compliment; he was screwing his eyes shut as Jakes took a corner at forty miles an hour, the car's tyres squealing. 'This is the way to Cawster. Why aren't we going straight back to Falbrough, Sergeant?'

'Because the sooner Chief Inspector Stubbs hears about this, the better, and we can phone from the station in Cawster. If he's not back, at least we can leave a message. And while we're there, we can ask around among the Cawster lads, and see if they know of anybody local who owns an old Daimler. That's a distinctive car, there can't be many in this area.'

'Maybe it wasn't from this area. Craggs had another little bombshell for us. He noticed something else that might help identify our villain.'

'Why didn't you say so before?' Jakes glanced at him, his mouth quirking. 'You're enjoying this, aren't you, Sherlock, spinning out your little tit-bits of information?'

Deepbriar shook his head. 'You keep jumping in before I have the chance to finish. Like I told you, Eddie Craggs and this chap had a bit of a scrap, and Eddie came off best, though it sounded as if he took a few hard knocks. Anyway, after a bit this bloke broke free and ran back to the car, and Eddie went after him. He was only seventeen, and he's not a big lad even now, so he showed a fair bit of nerve.'

'If you say so. Is there a point to this?' Jakes asked impatiently.

'Yes. The point is, Eddie saw a peaked cap lying on the passenger seat.'

'What?' The car swerved a little as Jakes yelped. 'Blimey! Which service?'

'Take it easy, Sergeant,' Deepbriar pleaded, squirming in his seat. 'The cap was nothing to do with the armed services. It was deep blue, and Craggs was pretty sure it belonged to a chauffeur's uniform. It certainly fits with the car.'

'Ye-es,' Jakes breathed. 'That's what I call

a lead! Hang on, though. Why would he have been wearing a hat, if he had a cap in the car?'

'A disguise? June said it hid his face,' Deepbriar said. 'And a uniform cap would be far more memorable; even a child would probably be able to describe it.' He sighed. 'The trouble is, there's still no link between this man and the two dead girls.'

'We know they were both taken away by car,' Jakes said. 'And they lived on the same side of the city. Not much, but it's enough of a connection. It's not as if we have any other leads worth chasing.'

Janey Smithers had been buried in a shallow grave, hollowed out next to a fox's earth, presumably in a deliberate attempt to prevent its discovery; the powerful scent of the animals almost masked the odour of decay. The site was in the depths of a remote valley which was used for rough grazing by a local farmer. It was his son, out to round up the sheep, who had found the body, led to the spot by his dogs. Half-expecting to find the carcass of a ewe, the young man went close enough to see a child's bare foot, protruding from a mound of newly disturbed earth.

It was Sergeant Gough who shared this information with Jakes and Deepbriar when they returned from their visit to Eddie Craggs.

'Chief Inspector Stubbs came back about an hour ago,' he said, when Jakes asked him. 'I gave him your message, but he was in a hurry, he had to meet Chief Superintendent Murray. He shouldn't be gone much longer.'

Constable Tidyman looked up from his work. 'You think finding Janey's body will provide any clues?' the young constable asked. 'Something that might help us work out who killed her?'

Jakes shrugged. 'Not unless the bloke was stupid,' he replied. 'But we'll get him,' he added grimly. 'We have to.'

'Nobody was caught for that other case though,' Tidyman said.

Before the sergeant could reply, Chief Inspector Stubbs came in. 'Ah, Jakes. I'm glad you're back.'

'Do you need me, sir?' Jakes asked.

'Probably.' The senior officer looked around. 'Deepbriar, why are you still here? Aren't you supposed to be moving house this afternoon?'

Deepbriar looked at the clock; it was already 1.30. 'Yes sir.' He didn't want to go, not when the case might really be getting somewhere. 'But there's our report...'

'I got your message,' Stubbs said dismissively. 'I'm not sure it's worth pursuing.'

Deepbriar opened his mouth to protest, but Jakes got in first. 'What about the information Thorny got from Eddie Craggs, sir? The incident in 1950 does have some similarities to this case.'

'What's the word of a convicted felon worth? If we had a more reliable witness it might be different; the girl who was molested, perhaps? But if she's from Carrside too, then I doubt if a court would trust her evidence either.'

'She's not from Carrside, and she seemed quite bright,' Jakes said. 'Admittedly she wasn't much help on what the man looked like, but Craggs gave us a very detailed description.'

'Sir, I think Craggs was telling the truth,' Deepbriar put in. 'He had no reason to lie, and he was pretty mad about his kid sister and her friend being attacked. And if the man he assaulted was an innocent victim, why didn't he complain about being attacked?'

Stubbs shrugged. He seemed to have lost heart. 'Who knows? There could be a dozen different reasons. Perhaps he'd just taken time off when he was supposed to be working. Even if everything happened the way Craggs says, there's still not much to connect this man with the two cases of murder. We don't have time to chase red herrings.'

Deepbriar looked an appeal at Jakes, but he could see the sergeant wasn't going to argue the point any further.

'You said you had something for me to do, sir?' Jakes said.

His expression grim, the chief inspector nodded. 'There's no doubt about the child's identity. Right now you and I have to go and break the news to Janey Smithers's parents.'

Deepbriar was suddenly more relieved than sorry to be leaving. As a village bobby he'd done his share of carrying bad news, but never anything quite so bad as this; in cases of violent death there was some advantage in being low down in the ranks. Sergeant Jakes met Deepbriar's eyes and shrugged as he followed Stubbs from the room. A sudden thought occurring to him, Deepbriar turned to Sergeant Gough.

'Exactly what message did you pass on to Chief Inspector Stubbs?' he asked.

Gough rummaged around on his desk and picked up a scrap of paper. 'There,' he said, handing it to the constable. Deepbriar read it out. *Rumour of 1950 assault appears true. Inmate of county prison admits chasing and beating up man who approached two girls, one of them his sister.* Thorny grimaced. 'Is that all you told him? What about the car Eddie saw, and the peaked cap on the seat?'

'My pencil broke,' Gough replied. 'Besides, Jakes was on his way back, and it was time for my lunch. There was no point taking down every little detail.'

Without a word Deepbriar dropped the scrap of paper on to Gough's desk and turned back to sit at his own. Jakes might have brought Stubbs up to date by now, but faced with the visit to Mr and Mrs Smithers he doubted it. More sure than ever that the attack on June Day was relevant, he pulled a sheet of paper towards him, took out his notebook, and began work on his report. Moving house would have to wait.

Deepbriar's reception when he eventually arrived home wasn't as bad as he'd expected. Since he'd already carried as many of their possessions to the new house as he could manage, there were only the essentials they'd been using and a few heavy pieces of furniture waiting to be transported, and by the time he reached Minecliff, at a quarter to three, most of them were already in the van. Mary was in the van as well, sitting in the passenger seat, knitting placidly. 'How did you get in there?' Deepbriar asked, opening the door and stretching up to give her a kiss.

'Johnny gave me a boost,' she said. 'He's the younger one. He says he'll help me down at the other end too; there's no need to worry. There's nowhere comfortable inside,' she explained, 'I shan't have to sit here much longer, anyway, I think they're nearly finished.'

'You haven't been working too hard, have you?' he asked, suspiciously. It was quite unlike her to rest while anyone else was working. 'You're all right?'

'Of course I am.' Mary made a start on a new row. 'I suppose you've got a good reason for being this late?'

'Yes, I was a bit busy, I'll tell you once we're all done here.' Deepbriar went into the house and found that three ladies from the WI were hard at work cleaning up. 'Who persuaded Mrs Deepbriar to behave herself?' he asked.

'That was Miss Cannon,' came the reply. The woman smiled. 'And it wasn't exactly persuasion, more like an order.'

He shook his head in disbelief. 'She's never obeyed an order from me,' he said.

The women exchanged glances that suggested they found nothing strange about that. Deepbriar sighed. Despite his long service in Minecliff his authority had diminished rapidly since he stopped wearing a uniform.

'Miss Cannon has gone on ahead with the rest of our volunteers. They're at the cottage, all ready and waiting.' There was a clatter of boots on the stairs and two men appeared, carrying a chest of drawers between them.

'Only the dresser to come,' the older man said. 'We're nearly ready for the off. You want a lift, Constable? With your missus in the front, Johnny will be sitting on the sofa inside, but there's room for two.'

'I've got my bike, thanks,' Deepbriar said, a little stiffly. 'I'll see you there.'

At number four Stellings Lane, Miss Cannon and three more members of the Women's Institute awaited the arrival of the van. 'This is very good of you,' Deepbriar said.

Miss Cannon, neat as always in her tweeds and with not a hair out of place, waved away his thanks. 'What are neighbours for? You don't need to worry, Constable, your wife won't be allowed to tire herself. Mary will have plenty of help to get settled. We shan't make a nuisance of ourselves, but there'll be somebody available if they're needed.'

The van arrived, with two pink-cheeked and giggly ladies squashed on the sofa with Johnny in the back, while the third rode her bicycle behind. With Deepbriar to help, the van was soon emptied. An hour later, fortified by tea and cake, the removal men duly departed.

Mary was installed in a comfortable chair wherever supervision was needed. Deepbriar assisted when he was able, but the ladies of the WI made it plain, with a good-natured tolerance, that they were quite able to cope on their own.

After a while Deepbriar wandered out into the garden. More than half his mind had stayed in Falbrough; he wished there had been a chance to report personally to Stubbs. Maybe the chief inspector had read his report, and by now the hunt for the Daimler would be under way.

There was no opportunity to talk to Mary until bedtime; they were sharing their bed once more, at her insistence. 'We can't start our life in a new home with you napping on the sofa,' she said. 'Think of it, Thorny, this house is all ours! Isn't it wonderful? I never thought we'd own a home of our own.' She gave him a brief hug, then pulled away as the baby kicked. 'I think Deepbriar junior is getting impatient, perhaps he wants a bedtime story. Tell us about your busy morning.'

'Fair enough, if you're not too tired.' Deepbriar began by relating the astounding news that the sudden death at Cripps & Jones hadn't been a murder at all. 'There'll be a few red faces over that,' he said, and waited for Mary's reply, only to hear a very soft snore from her side of the bed. He sighed. His wife, at least, would have a restful night, untroubled by the knowledge that little Janey Smithers's body had been found.

''Night, love,' Deepbriar muttered. He lay staring up at the unfamiliar ceiling; being in a different house after so many years would take some getting used to, and within a few days he would be a father. That event would change their lives even more; there would be new responsibilities to face. He tried to shake away the thought that while boys would always be boys, there would be even more to worry about if the baby turned out to be a girl.

'He never brought a car down here,' Deep-briar grumbled, as brambles snagged at his trouser legs. He was next in line to a uniformed constable, as part of a search team, detailed to find out how Janey Smithers had been taken to the place where she was found. The young man who discovered the body had assured Inspector Young that no vehicles could come anywhere near the old earth, but the inspector seemed determined to prove otherwise.

'I don't see why he'd bother,' the other man called back, flinging out his arms to regain his balance as he slipped on a stone. 'We can't be more than half a mile from the road, and a little girl wouldn't weigh much.'

'Depends how fit a man is, I suppose,' Deepbriar said, recalling how the boxes he had carried through the village a few nights before had grown heavier at each step. 'I wouldn't want to try it, not over rough ground like this.'

'If she was already dead, he'd have put her over his shoulder,' the constable said. 'I interviewed the woman who saw Janey get into the car, and she reckoned the man wasn't particularly tall, but he was solid like.'

'Did you hear that?' Deepbriar called, looking at Sergeant Jakes, who was supervising the row of officers snaking slowly across the valley, walking from one to another and encouraging them to keep their minds on the job. 'Remember what Eddie Craggs said about the man he chased?'

Jakes nodded and came closer. 'I know what's on your mind, Thorny,' he said, beating at a clump of drooping brambles with a stick, 'but realistically, all we've got is hearsay, most of it the word of a convicted felon.'

The two CID officers fell into step as they reached a clearer patch of ground. They had talked over this subject several times before. Chief Inspector Stubbs must have seen the report Deepbriar had left on his desk the previous afternoon, but they'd heard nothing from him, so presumably he'd been unimpressed.

'Sergeant, do you happen to recall the name of the builder?' Deepbriar asked.

'Which builder?' Jakes looked bewildered.

'The man who tried to follow the abductor's car.'

'Oh, him. Yes, he's quite well known in Cawster. His name's Dinsdale. He lives in Cedar Road, got a little yard there. Why do you want to know?'

The constable's cheeks flushed a little. 'Our house needs a bit of work doing. If putting in a bathroom isn't too small a job for him, I might try Dinsdale.'

'And while you're asking, he might not mind chatting about that car,' Jakes said, looking amused. 'I wish you luck, Thorny, I got the impression the man's as blind as a bat, so I hope you don't object to crooked walls.'

'He can't be that bad, or nobody would employ him.' They walked on in silence for a while, studying the ground, each busy with their own thoughts.

'I'd not want to be in the boss's shoes,' Jakes said suddenly. 'The chief super was on the phone again this morning; he wants results, and fast.'

'Wants miracles, more like.' It was the uniformed constable again, coming closer as he worked his way around a tangle of blackthorn. 'Does he think the blighter will have dropped his wallet, or left his coat hanging on a handy bush, complete with a name tag?'

'Stranger things have happened,' Jakes said. 'Anyway, we've got our orders.' He went to join a pair of men who had stopped to study something a hundred yards away.

As he lay wakeful the night before, Deepbriar had come up with several ideas; he would like to interview Eddie Craggs again. The car's registration hadn't been specifically mentioned, but there was just a chance he might remember something about it; even a single letter or number could be a help.

The morning dragged to an end. Lunch was a cup of tea, served up by the farmer's wife, along with sandwiches and a slab of cold pork pie, brought out from the station canteen. As they finished eating Inspector Young came to deliver his orders for the afternoon. 'We've drawn a blank from this end,' he said, 'so we'll try another approach. We'll split into two teams. Either the car came from the lane over there to the east, or past Everscombe. Sergeant Jakes, you and Deepbriar will take a group to walk the lane, and see if there are any signs of a car pulling off in this direction. Sergeant Gough and Constable Tidyman's detail will do the same thing along the main road.'

'And in the meantime he'll be sitting snugly by the fire with his feet up,' a voice whispered sourly in Deepbriar's ear. He turned to see Sergeant Gough, rubbing at his knee as if it was troubling him. The man limped off towards the inspector, pulling faces as if he was in considerable pain. A few minutes later Inspector Young came to tell Deepbriar that he would be in charge of the search party examining the road, as Sergeant Gough had sprained his leg.

'Lucky you spent all those years on the beat, eh Constable?' the inspector said. 'Keeps a man a lot fitter than sitting at a desk.'

Biting off a reply, Deepbriar nodded, and went to join Constable Tidyman. His young colleague was none too happy either, choosing to take it as a slight that he wasn't trusted to organize the detail by himself.

Cycling home some hours later, Deepbriar took a detour, going up the hill to the house where young Oliver Rose lived. Oliver had been a victim of polio, but at the beginning of September he had started to attend the village school, walking a mile a day despite the callipers on his legs. As he knocked at the door the constable reflected guiltily that it was a long time since he had called. He owed the boy a lot for the help he'd given in a previous case of murder, and now he was only here because he wanted to ask a favour.

Mrs Rose waved away his apologies and ushered him into the sitting room. A moment later Oliver's uneven tread could be heard coming down the stairs, accompanied by the pattering paws of his three-legged dog, Barney. The dog danced around Deepbriar, yapping enthusiastically, and the boy's face lit up when he saw the visitor. 'Mr Deepbriar! I hoped it was you.'

'I'm after your help again, Oliver,' Deepbriar admitted, bending down to scratch behind Barney's ear. 'I know you don't have much time to take down car numbers, not with being at school, but do you still have all those books about cars?'

'Yes, of course,' the boy replied, a touch of scorn in his voice. 'I haven't stopped being interested in cars.'

'I was wondering if you'd let me borrow a couple,' Deepbriar said. 'What I need are some pictures of big old saloon cars. Pre-war I think. Would you have such a thing?'

Oliver's eyes were suddenly very wide and round. 'Is this for a case?' he asked.

'That's right. I can't tell you all the details just now, but it's quite important.'

The boy nodded and almost ran from the room, and they heard his voice floating down to them as he dot-and-carried his way back up the stairs. 'I'll lend you *The Observer's Book,* and Dad found this really old magazine, from about 1937, and we cut out all the pictures and stuck them in a scrapbook. There's a Rolls Royce, and a Bentley...'

'I'll need some foreign ones as well,' Deepbriar called after him.

'Oh yes, there's a Mercedes Benz, and a Hispano Suiza, all sorts, you'll see.'

Chapter Nine

Deepbriar cycled to the end of Cedar Road, where a signboard told him he had found the right house. His knock brought a neat round-faced woman to the door.

'Good morning,' Deepbriar said. 'Can I speak to Mr Dinsdale?'

'I'm afraid you've missed him by about five minutes,' the woman said, 'but I can tell you where he's working this morning, if that's any help.'

With his eye on the town hall clock, Deepbriar pedalled quickly through the middle of Cawster; he had no wish to explain his lateness to Chief Inspector Stubbs. Another half-mile found him in a leafy side street, at the address Mrs Dinsdale had given him. A battered van stood outside the house; Deepbriar could see why the builder had failed in his attempt to keep up with the abductor's car.

Deepbriar propped his bike against the kerb in front of the van and peered through the windscreen, which was scratched and none too clean. Dangling from the steering wheel was a pair of spectacles, with lenses in the same state. One of them seemed about to detach itself from the frame. It was a wonder the builder had been able to see the car in front of him at all, and hardly surprising that his description had left a lot to be desired.

'Did you want something?' A short rotund figure in blue overalls had come out of the house, a toolbox in one hand and a length of guttering in the other. He stood squinting up at the constable, his eyes like bright black buttons pressed deep into his weathered face.

Deepbriar introduced himself, and explained his errand. 'I don't know if you take on that sort of job,' he said. 'It would only be a week or two's work.'

'I'm not that busy just now,' Dinsdale replied, pulling a notebook from his pocket, along with a stub of pencil. 'Hold on, don't I know you? Deepbriar you said? Yes, I remember. Minecliff. I repaired the roof of the pub, about five years ago. You're the village bobby.'

'I was, I'm with Falbrough CID now.'

'A detective? Are you working on that murder case? That poor little kid. I've been feeling proper bad about it. If only I'd been along a few minutes earlier, I might have been able to do something. As it was I didn't have a hope of catching up with the rotten blighter.' Dinsdale shook his head, reaching into his pocket for a notepad and a stub of pencil. 'Ah well, life goes on, as they say. Give me your address, and I'll call round and take a look at what you want done.'

Deepbriar couldn't help himself; his eyes wandered back to the ancient and battered spectacles, then to the house where Dinsdale had been working. A lean-to had been added to the side wall, and there was new pointing on the chimney breast.

'It's only at a distance I don't see so well, lad,' Dinsdale said drily. 'I only wear them glasses for driving the car.' As if to illustrate the point he wrote the name *Deepbriar* in a small neat hand, and looked up expectantly, waiting to be told the address.

Having given him the information, Deepbriar drew himself up to his full height. 'If I was on duty, Mr Dinsdale, I might warn you that you could be a danger to other drivers, with those glasses and your windscreen in that state.'

'My wife says the same thing,' Dinsdale replied placidly, 'but I've not had an accident in thirty years of driving. How would it be if I call round first thing on Monday?'

Deepbriar was hot and short of breath by the time he arrived at Falbrough police station, and his heart was beating a little faster than he liked, for his conscience was beginning to bother him. Before he asked Dinsdale to look at pictures of cars with an eye to identifying one of them, he really ought to clear it with his senior officer. Perhaps Chief Inspector Stubbs had read his report by now, and would agree to let him go on with his enquiries, or maybe some new evidence had appeared overnight.

It was a forlorn hope. Since the flurry of activity when Janey Smithers's body was found, the search for her murderer had lost impetus. They were going over the same ground, both physically and metaphorically. Deepbriar trailed behind Sergeant Jakes as he strode once more around the dead girl's neighbourhood, and once they returned to the station he reread countless statements and reports, but he found nothing new there.

Looking as if he hadn't slept for at least a week, Chief Inspector Stubbs gathered his officers together as the long afternoon drew to a close, and informed them that rest days were being reinstated. 'It's no good being so exhausted that you can't think straight,' he said. 'Those of us on duty tomorrow will continue the door to door enquiries. Sunday is a good time to catch up with the people who were out when we called before. I want the rest of you to take things easy, and be ready for a fresh start on Monday. That'll be all, thank you.'

As Stubbs turned to hurry away, Deepbriar bit at his lip, wondering if he should come clean and tell his superior what he planned to do, but the chief inspector was on his way to yet another meeting with Chief Superintendant Murray, and before Thorny could make up his mind to speak, the chance was gone.

It felt strange to have Sunday off, with nothing more taxing to do than a spell at the church organ. 'The rector will be pleased,' Mary said, as she packed him off early with a peck on the cheek. 'He was expecting to have to make do with Mrs King on the piano, and it really isn't the same.'

'So where's Bella?' Thorny asked, winding a scarf round his neck. 'Is she poorly?'

'No, there's a special service at Possington. It's two years since the organ at St Peter and St Paul's was restored. Father Michael asked her if she thought you'd be able to do it, but Bella told him how busy you were, chasing after poor little Janey's murderer.'

It was typical of Bella Emerson to add insult to injury by denying him a chance to play at Possington, Deepbriar thought, as he strode towards the church. He had been the main organist at All Saints in Minecliff until the wretched woman came to the village and stole his place. Admittedly it had been difficult occasionally, when his duties clashed with the times of services, but as a whole the arrangement had worked well. Now he had to be content with the crumbs dropped from Bella's table. On the rare occasions when he had the chance, playing the magnificent instrument at St Peter and St Paul's was like a banquet.

The rector met him at the vestry door welcoming him like a prodigal son, returning after an absence of years. 'Thorny, it's so good to see you. I've a fire in here, if you want to warm yourself up. Mrs Emerson keeps asking me to provide an electric fire in the organ loft, but I don't think she realizes how much they cost to run.' He gave a conspiratorial wink. 'Between you and me, I rather hope the winter weather might prove too much for her. I'd dearly like to offer you your old post back, if you were willing to take it.'

'I'm not sure, to be honest,' Deepbriar said, shedding his coat and scarf. 'It's more difficult to predict when I'd be available, now I'm with the CID. Makes me appreciate how much freedom a village bobby has.'

'I trust you aren't regretting the move?' Robert Pusey waved him to a chair in front of the log fire, and sat down in another.

'No, not exactly.' Thorny pulled a face. 'I'm not used to having somebody looking over my shoulder all the time. There are lines of enquiry which look worthwhile to me, but I can't act on them until I'm told. Not that I'm complaining; my boss is a good man, but he's got so much on his plate, especially in a case of murder.'

'That poor child. I can't stop thinking about her parents. We shall offer a prayer for them, of course, as I know many parishes will be doing, but I fear it's small comfort.'

Deepbriar nodded and changed the subject. 'How's the committee getting on with deciding how to spend Mrs Twyford's legacy? Any chance we'll get the organ renovated?'

'I live in hopes,' the rector replied. 'I'm afraid Mrs Emerson doesn't have your ability to hide the worst of the poor instrument's faults.'

Voices sounded outside and the Reverend Pusey rose. 'That will be the bellringers.'

'You won't mind if I start playing straight away?' Deepbriar asked, following him to the door. '*Sotto voce,* as it were, I'll not be audible over the bells. And I'll try to go easy if you think it's necessary.'

The rector smiled. 'You are more important than a mere assemblage of pipes and keys, Thorny, I imagine you need a little relaxation. Play whatever you choose, as long as you're engaged in something suitable when the congregation arrive.'

Nearly two hours later, Deepbriar entered the back door of the cottage to be welcomed by a fine aroma. Mary was nowhere to be seen, and he hurried upstairs, jolted back to his ever-present worries. The floorboards groaned under his tread as he reached the landing, and he recalled that he had promised to deal with them at the earliest opportunity. Perhaps the morning would have been better spent with a hammer and nails.

He found his wife in the bedroom. She was removing the dingy brown paper from the walls; the whole house needed redecorating, but they had decided this was the most urgent job, so that the room was fresh and clean when the baby was born.

'You don't regret us buying this place, do you, love?' he asked, taking the scraper from her hand and taking over the task.

'Of course not.' She recaptured the tool. 'You shouldn't do that in your decent clothes, Thorny, and dinner's nearly ready anyway. Why? You're not sorry we're here, are you?'

'Not exactly. But it's a lot of work. And even if Mr Dinsdale takes on the job, it could be weeks before we've got a proper bathroom.'

'Then we'll be like half the rest of Minecliff. The police house was nice enough, but even after all those years it was never ours, and never would be. I've only been in this cottage three days, and I love it already. It's a proper home. I don't care if it's a bit shabby to start with.' She steered him towards the wardrobe. 'Get changed, and come downstairs.'

146

Ignoring this command, he put an arm round her. 'You will be all right, won't you, Mary love? I mean, having the baby. Only, well, not that you're old, but...'

'If I had a penny for every time you've started worrying over nothing, we could have bought a house three times this size,' Mary declared, pulling free and giving him a shove. 'Hurry up, the joint will be ready to carve; you don't want it to spoil.'

'All right if I start on Wednesday?' Mr Dinsdale asked, running a professional eye over the ancient stonework that supported the remains of a leaking roof. 'Not much wrong with the walls. It won't take more than a day to get the old wood and slates down and cleared out of the way, then with that old loft wall built up about a foot, we can put a nice little room on top.' He pointed. 'We can open up that old doorway and Bob's your uncle.'

'That's fine. Look, can you spare a couple more minutes?' Deepbriar asked, as he led the way back inside. 'This isn't official, but it's about the Janey Smithers case. That car you tried to follow.' Oliver's books were laid out ready on the table. 'I thought you might recognize it from one of these.'

'I might at that,' Dinsdale agreed. There was silence as he leafed through the small book, shaking his head from time to time. He put it aside and moved on to the scrapbook. He'd only turned half a dozen pages when he stopped, pointing at a picture that covered more than half a page. 'Blow me! That's it, as near as dammit.'

The illustration showed the backs of two cars as one overtook the other on a steep mountain road. Since one was an open-topped sports model, it was obvious which one Dinsdale was talking about. There was nothing to indicate what make of car it was, but no doubt Oliver Rose would know.

'You're sure?' Deepbriar asked. 'Only it's important we get this right.'

'That's the shape,' Dinsdale nodded vigorously. He thumped a stubby forefinger on the picture of the sports car. 'Shame I wasn't driving that when I tried chasing him, eh?'

There was work waiting for Deepbriar back at the office; the files concerning the factory break-ins had been left on his desk again, this time with a note from Stubbs, asking the constable to work out why a crook was wasting his time with a few shillings from petty cash-boxes, when he had the skills to tackle something more rewarding.

'You drew the short straw then,' Sergeant Jakes remarked, seeing what Deepbriar was looking at when he came in.

'Did you try telling the chief about the attack on Annie Craggs and June Day?'

Deepbriar asked. 'Only I don't think he's had time to read my report.'

'He wasn't in the mood to listen,' Jakes said. 'I don't know, Thorny, maybe we were jumping to conclusions.'

Deepbriar didn't reply. By tomorrow morning perhaps he'd have at least one more piece of the puzzle in place. If Oliver Rose identified that picture as a Daimler, he'd see Stubbs in the morning and come clean. With only half his mind on the job, he spent the day going over all the reports concerning the break-ins. By 5.30 he had learnt a great deal about the factories that had been broken in to, and a little about the people who did their accounts, but absolutely nothing useful about the man who had robbed them.

With no other ideas in his head, he added up the sum total of money stolen; it barely added up to a month's wage. Why risk getting caught for so little return? As Deepbriar rose to leave, stretching to straighten the kinks out of his spine, a thought struck him at last. It was too late to do anything about it now, but if Chief Inspector Stubbs gave him permission he might try visiting one or two of the crime scenes the next day.

Barney came leaping around Deepbriar's feet as the door was opened; the dog was amazing agile on his three remaining legs. Mrs Rose smiled a greeting just as welcoming but less energetic. 'Come in, Thorny. Oliver's in the living room.'

There was a strong smell of beef and onions filling the house. 'I hope I'm not interrupting your meal?' Deepbriar asked.

'No, we shan't be eating for half an hour yet. You won't mind if I leave you with Oliver, though? I'm just doing the potatoes.' With this she ushered him through the living room door and closed it behind him.

'Sorry I didn't come to the door,' Oliver said, 'but I didn't want to lose track of what I'm doing.' He was building a complicated looking structure out of Meccano, with pieces strewn all over a small table. 'Are you any good at axles? Only this doesn't seem to turn properly.' For several minutes they put their heads together and worked on the project in near silence. Eventually the machine, which seemed to be a combination tractor and elevator, stood complete.

'It's very good,' Deepbriar said. 'Do you want to be an engineer when you grow up?'

'I'm not sure. I was wondering about being a vet. Or a detective, like you.' Oliver's eyes suddenly opened wider. 'Were my books any help?'

'I think they might have been. I've brought them back, but depending how much you can tell me about a certain picture, I might want to borrow them for a bit longer.'

The boy was almost bouncing out of his

chair in his excitement. 'That's all right. What did you want to know?'

Turning to the illustration Dinsdale had singled out, Deepbriar pointed to the car. 'What make is that?' he asked.

'It's a Daimler,' the boy replied.

'Are you quite positive?'

'Sure as sure. Hold on.' Oliver picked up the *Observer's Book* and turned the pages with practised ease. 'That's not exactly the same model,' he said, pointing to a photograph, 'but they're quite similar, though of course it's different seeing a side view. I'm not sure about the exact year this other one was built, but it was about 1930. The engine is...'

Deepbriar didn't listen as the boy rattled on. There was one more person he needed to talk to. He had to show this picture to the woman who had witnessed Janey Smithers's abduction.

Chapter Ten

Deepbriar walked into the CID office with Oliver's books in his hand. It was early, and the place was deserted, but the door to Chief Inspector Stubbs's room stood open, and he could see his senior officer seated at his desk. Squaring his shoulders, the constable knocked on the varnished wood, took a deep breath and went in.

'Sir...' he began, but Stubbs interrupted him.

'Did you find anything interesting on those factory break-ins, Thorny? Only the chief constable is taking an interest. He's getting some flak from the Chamber of Commerce.'

It took Deepbriar a moment to get his thoughts in order, for he had been thinking of nothing but the Janey Smithers case since he'd left the office the night before. 'Well, there must be something we're missing, sir, unless this chap is crazy. Do you mind if I visit the crime scenes again? There's an itch at the back of my mind, and taking a look round might bring it to the surface.'

The chief inspector almost smiled. 'It was your sixth sense that persuaded me you ought to be in the CID, but try telling that to anyone else and I'll deny I ever said it. I don't want to be put down as a crank.' He noticed the items Deepbriar was holding. 'What have you got there?'

'It's to do with the Janey Smithers case.' Deepbriar hurried on, before Stubbs could interrupt again. 'I have a confession to make. There's some work that needs doing on our little cottage and when it came to contacting a builder I decided to go and see Mr Dinsdale, the witness who followed the car. I had this idea. I'm sorry, but I was hoping you'd follow up the attack on Annie Craggs. I know you didn't think her brother's statement was reliable, but since he identi-fied the car, and gave us that information about the chauffeur's cap–'

'Hold on.' The chief inspector leant for-ward, holding up a hand to silence Deep-briar's rather disjointed flow. 'I didn't hear anything about a car, or a cap.'

'I believe Sergeant Gough didn't have time to take down the whole of Sergeant Jakes's telephone message, sir.' Deepbriar glanced at the littered desk. 'I left you a report, but I know you've been very busy. You won't have found time to look at it yet.'

Stubbs riffled through the layers of paper. 'My turn to apologize, Thorny,' he said, finding the sheet covered in the constable's handwriting, 'I've been busy, but that's no excuse. Look, go and fetch us both a cup of tea while I read this. And stop looking so worried, I doubt if we'll be demoting you to traffic duty just yet.'

Deepbriar couldn't feel so sanguine, but he hurried off to the canteen. When he walked back into the office, Chief Inspector Stubbs put down the report with a sigh.

'You were right to bring this to my attention, Constable,' Stubbs said heavily. 'I suppose now you've spoken to Dinsdale and found a connection.'

Deepbriar picked up the two books he'd left on the chair. 'I showed him these, sir, and asked if he could pick out the car that he followed on the day of Janey Smithers's abduction.' He leafed through the scrapbook. 'He identified this one.'

Stubbs pursed his lips. 'A Daimler. So, somebody made a mistake. You've got a nasty habit of showing up your superiors' shortcomings, Thorny. One of these days you'll do as much for me, and I'll wish I'd left you in Minecliff.'

Deepbriar could only hope Stubbs wasn't being serious. He'd had no intention of stirring up a hornet's nest when he'd got his teeth into Sergeant Parsons's rumour; it had simply been one of those puzzles he so enjoyed unravelling.

'Anything else?' Stubbs asked. 'If you've done any more sleuthing on your own initiative I need to know.'

'That's it, sir,' Deepbriar replied, standing rigidly to attention.

'Right. Relax, man. Sit down and drink your tea,' Stubbs said. 'Identical cars used for such similar crimes would be too much of a coincidence, despite the time in between.' He rose and went to the door, taking the books with him. 'Sergeant Jakes, I've got a job for you. Take these over to Cawster and show them to the woman who witnessed Janey's abduction. Ask if she can find a car that looks like the one she saw.'

Jakes looked doubtful. 'I've read her statement, sir, and I don't think she'll be much help. She said the car was big, but she knows nothing about the different makes.'

'She doesn't need to know what they're called, to be able to recognize a shape,' Stubbs said impatiently. 'No giving her any clues, mind. While you're gone I'll get enquiries started among the local garages.'

'What would you like me to do, sir?' Deepbriar asked.

'You carry on with your work on the break-ins. They're closer to home and you can manage without a car. You're off the Smithers case for a day or two, and you'd better keep away from Chief Superintendent Murray; he was none too pleased about a lowly constable being best man at a society wedding when he wasn't even invited.'

'It wasn't a society affair,' Deepbriar

155

protested. 'There weren't more than thirty guests sitting down for the breakfast, and all of them were family or old friends.'

Stubbs looked amused. 'If the right opportunity crops up I'll tell him that; perhaps it will be some consolation. Go ahead and visit these crime scenes this morning. You've done a good job rooting out the Annie Craggs affair, Thorny, I won't deny it, but in future, check with me first, all right?'

'Yes, sir. I'm sorry. I didn't intend to go behind your back, it just sort of happened.' He left the office feeling as if a great weight had been lifted from his shoulders, but as he saw Jakes's desk he recalled that the sergeant had been entrusted with Oliver's precious books. He sprinted out to the yard, where he found his young colleague about to leave, but Jakes brought the car to a halt as Deepbriar flagged him down.

'What's up, Thorny?' The sergeant grinned. 'Are you being sent to ride shotgun?'

'No, I just wanted to ask you to take good care of those books. They belong to a young friend of mine, and he wants them back in one piece.'

Jakes nodded. 'I'll guard them with my life. So, are you on the trail of the Daimler?'

'No, but the chief's getting it started. I only hope I haven't got this all wrong.'

'There's no pleasing you, is there?' Jakes's smile widened as he lifted his foot off the clutch, and the rest of his words came to Deepbriar above the roar of the engine as the car pulled away. 'You were worried because your lead wasn't being investigated. Now it's official and you're fretting in case you've made a mistake!'

Thankful that he didn't have to endure another journey with Jakes, Deepbriar fetched his bicycle, pulling up his collar as a drizzle of rain started. A bus passed by, threatening to give him a soaking as it splashed through a water-filled pothole; there was something to be said for cars. His mouth turned down at the thought; the driving lessons had been temporarily forgotten, but he couldn't keep putting them off.

Coming to the entrance of Corders Machine Parts, the first of the factories on his list, Deepbriar fumbled in his pocket for his warrant card; he still wasn't used to his status as a plain-clothes policeman, and he half-expected the girl at the desk to argue when he asked to see the accounts manager.

'Oh, is it about the burglary?' She gave him a friendly smile. 'They didn't take much. I don't think Mr Trevor was too worried. Mr Trevor's in charge of our accounts department.'

'Yes, I know,' Deepbriar said. 'Is he in?'

Corders' petty-cash-box had been robbed of one pound, seventeen shillings and fourpence, plus stamps to the value of eight

157

shillings and fivepence halfpenny. Neither the drawer where the stamps were kept, nor the cash-box, had been locked.

'You don't use that for small amounts,' Deepbriar commented, nodding towards the safe standing in one corner of the accounts office.

'We do now,' Trevor told him. 'Though it's a bit of a palaver having to open up just to get a couple of shillings for tea and biscuits. It was an odd business. See that window? The thief forced it open, but the frame was hardly damaged. When we came in on the Tuesday morning, it was pushed shut, and everything was so tidy, you'd hardly know he'd been here.'

'Yes, he's not a messy villain, whoever he is,' Deepbriar replied. He walked across to the filing-cabinet. 'What do you keep in here?'

'Invoices and customer details in the top two drawers, staff records in the third, tax and national insurance and so on, and miscellaneous at the bottom.'

'Nothing particularly confidential?'

'Well, of course, we don't let just anybody come looking at our personnel files and accounts.' The man sounded slightly shocked.

'No, of course not,' Deepbriar said hurriedly. 'I was thinking of things that could be of value to somebody outside the company. Trade secrets, perhaps? New designs?'

'We'd have nothing like that in here,'

Trevor said. 'Do you think that's what the thief was after?'

'I've no idea, but I find it hard to believe he went to so much trouble for the sake of a couple of pounds in cash and stamps.' Deepbriar thought back to what he'd read in the file on the case. The detective sent to investigate had been thorough; he had asked the other office staff to check their desks and files, and had been assured that nothing was missing.

He shook his head, as if hoping this would jolt his brain into action. There had to be some other reason for this robbery and all the others; he simply had to work out what it was. 'Is it all right if I have a look round?' he asked.

'Yes, I should think so.' Trevor consulted his watch. 'I'm off to the bank in a minute, but Mrs Gooding will take care of you. The constable is to have whatever help he needs, Mrs Gooding, I'll be back in an hour.'

Once they were alone the prim little middle-aged clerk hovered beside the constable, looking nervous. Deepbriar gave her a reassuring smile. 'What I was wondering,' he said, 'was whether the thief was really thorough, or if he found the cash, grabbed it and ran.' It was a question Trevor had already answered, but he was interested to hear if Mrs Gooding agreed with her boss.

'He searched the whole office,' the woman

159

said decidedly. 'Everything was still quite neat, but I could tell.'

'Might I ask how?'

'Well, I like things in their proper places.' She opened a drawer and pointed to a glass jar containing paper clips. 'This pot had been moved; it was resting on the pad of paper underneath. And that ruler was lying flat, instead of being on its side against the ink bottle.'

'I see. You're a very observant person, Mrs Gooding. I imagine you have a good memory too.'

'I'm afraid not. Mr Trevor is a marvel. He never needs to look up telephone numbers, or the names and addresses of clients; it's all in his head.'

'You won't mind if I pretend to be the thief and look through the drawers and cabinets?' Deepbriar asked, and the woman shook her head.

'Would you like a cup of tea?' she asked timidly. 'Only it's almost the time when I usually go and make one for Mr Trevor, and he did say I was to look after you.'

'That would be very nice. Thank you, Mrs Gooding. Two sugars please.'

With a nod, as if happy at being given something familiar to do, she left. Deepbriar went through both desks with care, then examined a row of books and ledgers in a cabinet. Mrs Gooding came back with a tray, and began busying herself with the milk jug.

'Do you think the intruder looked in here?' Deepbriar asked.

'Yes, I'm certain he did.' Mrs Gooding nodded. 'What are you looking for?'

'I'm not too sure. The question is, what did our villain hope to find?'

As he closed the door of the cabinet an old telephone directory with a broken spine fell off the top, landing open at the first page. There were what looked like random numbers scribbled in all the unprinted areas, and Deepbriar smiled as he picked the book up. 'I sometimes do that, jot the number down once I've found it in the book.'

'I'm afraid I'm the culprit,' Mrs Gooding confessed. 'It's not just phone numbers either, I've got a very bad memory.'

Deepbriar went on with his search. After nearly an hour, he was none the wiser, and he decided it was time to move on.

Cripps & Jones was the next victim on his list, but that particular crime scene had been picked over inch by inch when it was thought the old watchman had been murdered, so Deepbriar doubted if anything would have been missed. He cycled instead to Fielders Pickles, on the outskirts of town. A strong scent, only slightly dampened by the drizzle, told him he was getting close. He was pedalling alongside a high brick wall, topped with broken glass. According to the reports, four weeks ago their mysterious thief had scaled this formidable barrier in order to reach the firm's offices, leaving with the princely sum of three pounds and twopence.

Fielders' had no separate accounts office. The people doing the paperwork shared a huge room with the packing and dispatch departments. Deepbriar received a noisy and excited welcome, which reminded him very much of the reception he got when he entered an infant school. There were actually only four women engaged on clerical tasks, while over a dozen more were sorting, labelling, and boxing the jars of pickle.

'It can't be easy to concentrate in here,' the constable remarked, having been offered a chair by the accounts clerk, a cheerful, spotty youth by the name of Loughbury. The ladies returned to their work, and calm was restored.

'You get used to it,' the clerk said. 'At least it's not boring. We thought the police had forgotten all about that robbery. Nothing much was taken.'

'No, but there's been quite a spate of these crimes.' Deepbriar looked around at the chaotic scene. 'I don't suppose it would be possible to tell in a place like this, but do you think the thief spent a lot of time in here? Could you tell if the contents of the drawers and filing cabinets had been disturbed?'

'I'm not sure. Though now you mention it,

Miss Williams was really relieved to find her watch was still where she'd left it. Hold on.' He leant backwards in his chair and called over one shoulder. 'Daphne, can you spare a mo?'

A pretty girl in a blue suit came hurrying across to them, giving the spotty young man a brief smile before transferring it to Deepbriar. 'Hello. This is all very exciting. Is it about the robbery again?'

'Yes. Mr Loughbury tells me your watch was left in the office that night.'

'That's right.' She fiddled with the watch on her wrist. 'I always take it off when I use the accounts machine, because it tends to shake down over my hand, and I put it in the drawer out of the way. Usually I remember to put it on before I go home, but I was in a hurry that day because I had a date, and I forgot. I was ever so glad to find it hadn't been taken.'

'Yes, that must have been a relief. So, the thief just searched until he found the cashbox...' Deepbriar began, but Daphne Williams broke in.

'That wouldn't have taken much doing,' she said. 'It always stood there, on top of the safe.'

Deepbriar looked. Fielders' safe was huge, the largest he'd ever seen, outside of a bank, and it looked brand new. 'That's a very fancy-looking object,' he said.

'It has a time lock,' Loughbury said, with as much pride as if he had designed the mechanism himself. 'Once it's closed for the night, the makers say it would take a hydrogen bomb to get it open again before the strike of nine the next day.'

'Very impressive. Can I have a look?'

'It's in the half-lock state now,' Loughbury explained, 'which means the combination will open it. I'll show you.' He turned his back, twiddled the dial a few times, then swung the door of the safe open. 'That's the timing mechanism,' he said, pointing. 'Either Mr Fielder himself or one of the managers will set that just before we close for the night. At the end of the last shift on Saturday it's locked up tight until Monday morning.'

The lock on the huge metal box looked to be far beyond the capabilities of a local safecracker. 'Would it be all right if I wander around the office?' Deepbriar asked. 'I'm trying to get a feel of what our villain was after. In most cases he seems to have gone through every single desk and cabinet.'

'Well, this place does look a bit chaotic. Perhaps that put him off,' Loughbury said. 'Go ahead. I'll be here if you want me again.'

With the necessary explanations to make at every desk, it took Deepbriar a long time to work around the whole room, but at last he returned to Loughbury, his notebook in his hand.

'It seems there's quite a bit that could have been stolen but wasn't,' he said. 'There's a silver penknife in the top drawer there,' he continued, pointing to the one desk that wasn't currently occupied. 'That must be worth a few pounds. I'm surprised it wasn't taken. Unless the knife wasn't here that night.'

'It's always there,' Loughbury said. 'It belongs to Mr Midgely, but we all borrow it.'

'Then there were stamps held by the dispatch department, valued at between eight and twelve pounds, so the young lady tells me, which are kept in an unlocked cupboard.'

Loughbury looked a little uncomfortable. 'We're supposed to collect those every afternoon and put them in the safe,' he admitted, 'but dispatch often work a bit later than the rest of us, if there's a special order to finish.'

'I suggest you change the system,' Deepbriar admonished. 'That's just asking for trouble. One more item. A Miss Kelly claims she is in the habit of hiding cash in the bottom drawer of her desk. Luckily the pound note she'd left that night wasn't found either. I have advised her that she should find a safer place for her savings.'

Loughbury nodded. 'She did tell me once that she leaves her spare money there until she gets round to putting it in the post office, but I didn't know it was ever as much as that.'

'All in all,' Deepbriar concluded, 'I think we can safely say that this place wasn't given the same treatment as the others.' But why not? he wondered, as he cycled back to the police station, his stomach beginning to rumble hungrily. According to the report, the thief hadn't been disturbed, but if he'd heard a particularly noisy vehicle pull up in the road outside, it might have sounded as if it was entering the yard. The constable lowered his head against the rain, which had turned from drizzle to downpour, and turned his thoughts instead to the beef sandwiches Mary had prepared for him; they would taste even better with a few dollops of pickle added. There was a jar in his saddlebag, courtesy of Mr Fielder himself. It was against the rules of course, accepting gifts from the public, but to refuse would surely have given offence.

Chapter Eleven

Chief Inspector Stubbs was out. Nobody else had any information for Deepbriar, and after he'd eaten his lunch he visited the sites of two more break-ins, but pedalling home at the end of the day, he felt no wiser. There had been no sudden enlightening flash of inspiration. As far as he could tell, only Fielders hadn't been thoroughly searched, while at all the other crime scenes small items had been stolen, and the contents of desks and cupboards had been disturbed, albeit only to a small degree.

With a general feeling of dissatisfaction, Deepbriar found himself at home, hardly aware of having made the journey. There was still that itch at the back of his mind, but it was so vague that he couldn't even be sure whether the feeling was connected to the Janey Smithers case or the robberies.

'I'm up here, love.' Mary's voice drifted from upstairs when he called her name. 'If you make a pot of tea I'll be down in a minute.'

Five minutes later he sat looking at his wife, a cup of tea nursed between his hands. There were lines around Mary's mouth that usually only appeared when she had a headache, but he knew better than to ask how she was; he felt too fragile to face her disapproval. He sighed, stretched his legs out under the table, and did his best to look cheerful. 'Had a good day?'

'I've finished stripping the wallpaper. How about you?'

It was all the prompting he needed. Thorny poured out his troubles. Although by the end of the recital he still had no answers, he felt better; once he'd got his worries out in the open Mary reminded him, with her usual common sense, that he was only one man. He didn't have to find Janey Smithers's murderer all on his own. Half of Falbrough's CID officers were trying to track down the Daimler and its chauffeur, so it wasn't as if the case had hit a dead end. Only the factory break-ins remained his sole responsibility, and they were hardly a matter of life and death.

On Wednesday morning Dinsdale turned up early in his battered van. It was being driven by his son, who bore a great resemblance to his father, being equally short and round, but with more hair. 'I'm having my eyes tested tomorrow,' the builder confided. 'The wife's been giving me grief about those glasses for weeks. Blow me if she didn't go and drop the danged things yesterday.' He pulled the mangled remains of the ancient spectacles from his pocket and inspected them ruefully. 'Made a proper danged job of it, too.'

'Just as well,' Thorny said, watching from the doorway as the men began to unload their tools. 'Mrs Deepbriar's inside, she'll keep you supplied with tea.' He lowered his voice as the older man came by again. 'I'd be grateful if you'd not let her come clambering over the rubble.'

Dinsdale nodded. 'I'm not blind, nor daft. Due soon, eh? Don't fret lad, we'll keep our eyes on her and fetch the tea things the minute she comes to the door.' He suddenly became very interested in the ladder which his son was lifting from the roof of the van. 'Careful with that, boy, you'll have the window out.'

Thorny turned, to find that Mary was standing at his side. There was a small frown between her eyes; he realized she looked no better than she had the day before. 'I thought you were in a hurry to get to work, Thorny,' she said, a little tartly he thought.

'Just going to get my bike,' he said, moving away, but something in her expression made him falter. 'You're all right?'

'Of course. Don't start your silly worrying again. There's no need for you to bother yourself about me. Aggie's coming over this morning, and if you don't move yourself, you'll be getting under our feet. Go on, get off and catch that villain.'

'But you'll send Aggie to the telephone if you need me to come home?' he persisted. Mary's sister was inclined to the view that men were an unnecessary evil around the house; he wasn't sure he trusted her to send for him if the baby decided to arrive.

Mary flapped an impatient hand at him. 'Stop fussing! Go to work, before I get really cross and your son gets upset; he's been nice and quiet so far this morning.'

Still a trifle uneasy, Deepbriar obeyed. He cycled to town and yet again his thoughts were miles away; luckily the lanes were quiet, and it wasn't until he reached Falbrough that a bus hooted impatiently to drag him out of his reverie, the driver shouting an insult because he was dawdling in the middle of the road.

He was just removing his cycle clips when Chief Inspector Stubbs called him. 'This one's yours, Deepbriar,' he said, handing the constable a slip of paper. 'Hobsons Brush Works; somebody broke in between midnight and six this morning. I'd hoped our eccentric thief had been scared off after all the fuss at Cripps and Jones, but it looks as if he's at it again.'

Deepbriar nodded. He knew he had no right to ask, but he simply had to know. 'The Daimler, sir, has anything been found?'

'You're to concentrate on these robberies,

Constable,' Stubbs said, a slight emphasis on the last word. 'We've all the manpower we need on the Smithers case. I'm relying on you to find our irrational thief.'

Deepbriar felt a flush come to his face. 'Sorry, sir. I'll get over to the brush works.'

Stubbs relented. 'We're following half a dozen leads, Thorny, but nothing concrete. By the time you get back, there may be some news.'

At the brush works, Deepbriar was met by the manager, Mr Ingles.

'You don't have a lot of security,' Deepbriar commented. The main gate was made of wood so ancient that it looked as if a puff of wind would blow it away.

'It's the first time we've ever been robbed,' the manager replied, making it sound like an accusation. 'The offices are kept locked, and there's no money here overnight.'

'Not even on payday?'

'No. We fetch the wages from the bank on a Friday morning, and pay our people the same night. To be honest, I wouldn't have bothered to call the police in, not over four shillings in petty cash, but Miss Stillbraith, our typist, was organizing a Christmas outing for the staff, and she'd collected over five pounds. She was keeping it in a tin in her drawer, silly girl. That's been taken.'

'What about damage done during the break-in?'

Ingles's face coloured slightly. 'There wasn't any. A window was left open overnight.'

Deepbriar looked suitably severe, although he doubted if shutting the window would have kept this particular villain out. 'You'd better show me, and I'll need to see where the money was.'

Studying the office, Deepbriar tried yet again to put himself in the intruder's shoes. The tin holding the money for the outing had been at the very back of a drawer, and hidden under a heap of papers, so once again the thief had made a meticulous search. The constable turned round slowly, and then stopped. This place had one thing in common with Cripps & Jones; their safe was exactly the same make and model. He shook the thought away; the thief had never even attempted to break into a safe, and he'd been told this one was hardly used.

Deepbriar interviewed Miss Stillbraith, who sat dabbing at reddened eyes. 'It's my fault, I suppose,' she said, 'but I didn't like to take the money home. I don't know what I'm going to do, everybody will be so disappointed, and it's all my fault.'

'Well, you couldn't have known there was going to be a break-in,' Deepbriar consoled, 'although you should have asked your boss to lock the money in the safe.'

'I didn't like to bother him. Do you think

you'll be able to get it back?'

'We'll do our best,' Deepbriar said, though privately he considered it was a forlorn hope; they were no nearer finding the thief than they'd been after the very first robbery, and once again there were no clues. What they needed was a huge slice of luck.

As he questioned the rest of the staff, several times Deepbriar found his gaze drawn to the safe. Of all the victims, only Fielders had one with a modern locking system. All the rest were quite antiquated, opened by a simple combination, or with a key. And Fielders' office hadn't been searched. A dull beginning of a light began to shine in some obscure corner of his mind, but before he could track it to its source he was interrupted.

'Have you finished?' Ingles asked, looking curiously at Deepbriar, who was standing with his mouth slightly open.

The constable shook himself. 'Nearly. Who knows the combination of your safe?'

'Let's see. There are five of us.' He listed them: himself, and the assistant manager, two people who were in charge of the accounts, and a secretary. 'But I told you, it's rarely used, and it doesn't look as if anyone tried to open it last night.'

'No,' Deepbriar mused, 'I can see that. Thank you for your cooperation, sir. We'll be in touch if there's anything else we need to know.'

At the tyre factory, his last call of the morning, the story was the same as before; little had been taken. With the firm's secretary hovering nervously at his elbow, Deepbriar stood in front of the large and rather battered looking safe that stood open in one corner. This model was old, and it was secured by nothing more complicated than a large key.

'How many people hold keys to the safe?' Deepbriar asked.

'I have one,' the secretary said, 'and the manager.' He looked a little uncomfortable. 'I know it isn't a good idea, but we leave a third hidden in the office. It gets so complicated if the manager and I are both off at the same time, but occasionally it's unavoidable. Anyway, the man who broke in didn't find our hiding place.'

'Hmm.' Deepbriar mused. 'Are you sure about that?'

The man looked surprised. 'Yes. The safe was still locked, and the key was where it belonged.'

'Show me,' Deepbriar said. He was led to a cupboard, where the secretary moved aside a pile of boxes to reveal the key hanging on a hook screwed into the wall.

'As you say, not a good idea; it would be safer in the hands of another member of staff.' The constable consulted his notes.

'Was anything stolen out of here?'

'Yes, we kept a torch on that shelf, in case of power cuts. I've asked everyone in the office, and they're sure it was there yesterday.'

'So, he searched this cupboard.' Knowing his methods, it seemed unlikely that the thief hadn't noticed the key. 'Do you keep the wages in the safe overnight?'

'Yes. We make up the pay packets on Thursday, ready to be handed out on Friday.'

The thief had never struck at the end of the week, Deepbriar reflected, cycling slowly back to the police station, lost in thought. If he'd noticed that key, surely he couldn't resist the temptation to look in the safe? It was almost as if he wasn't interested, but why not?

Jakes was at his desk when Deepbriar returned to the office. 'All right, Thorny?'

'No, something's niggling at me. Have you got a minute?'

'As long as you're quick, I've got three more garages to visit.'

'What do you know about breaking into a safe?' Deepbriar asked.

'Depends on the type,' Jakes said. 'There are some that don't need much more than a crowbar, but more modern ones are difficult, even for an expert. What's on your mind?'

'I'm not sure.' He explained about the key to the safe. 'He must have seen it, he pokes into every drawer, opens files and books, so why not use that key and take a look in the safe, even if it was only out of curiosity?'

The sergeant shook his head. 'He's a nut-case, that's the only answer I can come up with. I'm sorry, Thorny, but I have to go.'

Dispirited, Deepbriar ate a solitary lunch before settling down to pore over his notes yet again. At the end of the afternoon Jakes returned, closely followed by Chief Inspector Stubbs. In answer to Stubbs's question, Deepbriar confessed that he was no further forward in his investigations.

'Don't worry about it, Thorny,' Stubbs said. 'You're not the only one to draw a blank. It's late, get off home. Maybe tomorrow I'll find you a job on the Smithers case. We're not getting anywhere with the garages.'

'Maybe the murderer isn't local,' Deepbriar said, putting on his coat and hat.

'But he's been in the area at roughly the same time of year on three different occasions,' Sergeant Jakes pointed out. 'The attempted attack on Annie and June happened in October, too. If he doesn't live around here, he must have some other reason for being in the locality.'

'Yes, but where does that get us?' Chief Inspector Stubbs said. 'Perhaps we need to find a man who has a set routine, but who is he? Travelling salesmen don't have chauffeurs.'

'Hold on, maybe we're asking the wrong

question here,' Jakes said. 'This is a big posh car. What do wealthy men get up to in October that takes them away from home?' He looked questioningly at Deepbriar, who had paused in the doorway.

Thorny's eyes widened. 'Hunting, shooting and fishing,' he said.

'Blood sports,' Jakes concurred grimly.

Although it was late and Deepbriar was eager to get back to Mary, at Stubbs's request he called at Minecliff Manor on his way home. Colonel Brightman no longer rode to hounds, but he remained active among the shooting and fishing fraternity.

'Hello, Thorny.' It was Charles who greeted Deepbriar when he was shown into the drawing room at the manor. 'I suppose it's too early to offer you a drink?'

'I'm still on duty,' Thorny said. 'My boss asked me to speak to Colonel Brightman, so this is an official visit. Anyway, I mustn't be long, Mary will be expecting me.'

His friend gave him a look he couldn't interpret, but before Deepbriar could ask what was wrong, the door opened and Colonel Brightman came in. 'Evening, Thorny. Everything all right?'

'Yes, thank you, Colonel, but I've been given a job I'm not too sure how to tackle. My boss wants me to ask you for information about local sporting parties. Well, it's more about the people who come to them, really.'

'I'll help if I can,' the colonel said. 'What's the problem?'

Deepbriar launched into the story of the cap seen in the Daimler, and the theory that their suspect's employer came to the area to shoot. He put a hand in his pocket. A mechanic at one of the garages Jakes had visited that day had unearthed a picture of a Daimler which looked very similar to the one in Oliver's book. 'This is what we're looking for.'

'Hmm, I'm not much of an expert on cars,' Colonel Brightman said, shaking his head. 'Never been interested, to tell the truth. More your department, Charles.'

'I remember seeing a car like that, but it was a long time ago, and it wasn't near here.' Charles moved across to the sideboard to pour three measures of whisky. 'Tell Mary I forced it on you,' he said, as Deepbriar hesitated, 'Strictly for medicinal purposes; it's cold out.'

Deepbriar took the glass but didn't drink. 'The car, Charles,' he prompted.

'I doubt if it's any help. A friend of mine came to see me when I was stationed near Salisbury. Jack Hingham. He'd resigned his commission a couple of months before, and came to catch up on the old crew. He was driving a car exactly like that one.'

'Would that be Sir John's boy?' the colonel

said. 'Sir John Hingham comes north to shoot most years, not here, but on the Beckley estate. There's a chance you could be on to something. He definitely has a chauffeur.'

Deepbriar fetched out his notebook and wrote the name down. He couldn't help feeling a faint stir of excitement. 'Can either of you give me his address?'

Once he'd taken down what little they knew, he took a sip of the whisky, enjoying its warmth as the spirit slipped down his throat. As he drank a second mouthful the door opened. Elaine came in and her face lit up at the sight of him.

'Thorny. Are we celebrating? You might have called me, Charles. I did wonder, but I imagined it wouldn't be just yet...' she broke off, seeing the look of total confusion on Deepbriar's face. 'Oh heavens, I've put my foot in it. You've not been home.' Before he could say a word she hurried on. 'I'm so sorry. You know what the village is like, only when I went to the shop about lunchtime I heard that Mary's sister had called the midwife.'

It looked as if every light in the cottage was on. Deepbriar dropped his bike at the door and ran inside, to be met in the kitchen by Aggie. She blocked his way, arms crossed over her ample bosom. 'Mary's all right,' his sister-in-law said. 'But I don't think you'll

179

be allowed up there at the moment.'

'The midwife's with her, then?'

'Yes, she's been here on and off since twelve.'

'You should have telephoned me,' Deepbriar said, looking past her towards the stairs.

'Mary didn't want us to bother you. Take my word, there'll be nothing happening for a few hours yet, probably not until the morning. These things take time, especially when it's the first.' Aggie moved to the range then, where the kettle hissed quietly. 'There's a stew in the oven. I'll just make a pot of tea, and then I'd better get off home. You know where to find me if I'm wanted later, but if I don't hear from you I'll be back in the morning.'

'When can I go and see Mary?'

'I'll pop up and ask, while this is brewing,' Aggie replied placidly. 'When I came down she said to tell you not to fret, though heaven knows I'm wasting my breath.' She offered him a smile, which looked like one part sympathy and three parts exasperation. 'Sit yourself down, I already told you, it's far too soon to start pacing the floor.'

Ten minutes later Deepbriar was allowed to see his wife for a few unsatisfactory moments, with the midwife hovering in the doorway, and Mary clearly not wanting him to stay. Back downstairs he wandered disconsolately around the small rooms for

180

several minutes; they seemed suddenly very empty. A sensation under his belt buckle reminded him of what Aggie had said about his meal. He didn't think he was hungry, but once he'd lifted the pot on to the table the enticing smell of mutton stew tempted him to a small portion. This was followed by two more. With the inner man settled, it was a little easier to sit still. He pulled the chair close to the stove and picked up the newspaper.

Deepbriar had hardly read a word before his thoughts wandered. He was tormented by guilt; he'd been so thrilled at the prospect of being a father that he had given scant consideration to Mary, and the risks involved in giving birth. A first child at her age could be difficult. His natural pessimism led his meanderings swiftly to the worst possible outcome; Mary had been his rock for so many years, and as he began to imagine how dreadful his life would be without her, his spirits plummeted.

Gusts of rain were driving against the windows, and thunder rumbled in the distance; it was setting in for a wild night. Deepbriar turned on the wireless, but he could hardly hear it for the sound of the storm. Even when the thunder passed on the reception was bad, the signal broken up by the crackle of electrical interference. He soon reached to switch it off again.

With his feet propped up on a stool, Deepbriar drifted into an uneasy sleep. When he roused, with a crick in his neck and one hand frozen by the draught that edged in under the door, the rain was still drumming on the window. It was just after ten o'clock. He strained his ears for some sound from above, and thought he could hear the murmur of voices. He got to his feet and, stamping the cramp out of them, he went to the foot of the stairs, wondering if he might dare venture further. A heavy knock on the front door stopped him in his tracks.

He could think of no reason for anyone to be there at such an hour. Crossing the room in two strides, Deepbriar flung himself at the front door and pulled it wide. A man in shirtsleeves stood there, soaked to the skin, hair plastered flat to his head.

'Constable Giddens!'

The young policeman blinked rain from his eyes, his expression nearly as wild as his appearance. 'I need your help,' he said desperately. 'There's a child missing.'

Chapter Twelve

Deepbriar dragged the young constable inside, guiding him to the range, where a puddle of water swiftly began to form on the floor. Deepbriar handed Giddens a towel before turning to the kettle; the pot stood ready-charged with tea leaves, and it was but the job of a minute to put a steaming mug into the young man's shaking hands.

'You have to learn to put your cape on before you rush out,' Deepbriar said, 'no matter what the emergency might be. You're no good to the village if you come down with pneumonia. Now, sit yourself down and tell me what's happened.'

Pulling himself together, Giddens told the story quickly and succinctly. Deirdre Grigs-dyke hadn't come home from school that afternoon. At first nobody had been overly concerned; evidently she often went to a friend's house for an hour or two without going home first. She was still missing as darkness began to fall, and her brother was sent to fetch her, only to be told that Deirdre hadn't been there. Not only that, but she hadn't returned to school after lunch. Apparently, her brother had been the last person to see her. As usual they had eaten together in the kitchen, both their parents being out, but he had finished his sandwiches quickly and left early, wanting to play football before the first lesson.

On being told the news when he returned home, Alf Grigsdyke called on Miss Porter, Deirdre's teacher, who confirmed that the little girl had been absent that afternoon. She hadn't been worried; Deirdre was a sensible child, quite capable of summoning a neighbour if she felt seriously unwell. Alf fetched his bike and widened the search; he had a brother in Possington, and it occurred to him that Deirdre might have gone to see her cousins. Drawing a blank there, Alf went to every other place he could think of. At 9.30, with all other avenues explored, he had at last gone to the police house and called out Constable Giddens.

'She'd been gone eight hours by then, Thorny,' the young constable said, draining his mug. 'I went to the house, just in case she'd turned up, but she hadn't. Some of the neighbours had turned out, hearing all the commotion. Two of them said there'd been a car in the village about lunchtime, one they didn't recognize. I couldn't help thinking about what happened to little Janey Smithers. If only the kid's parents hadn't wasted so much time.'

Deepbriar grimaced. 'They aren't the kind

to worry overmuch, and calling in the police isn't their way. I take it you've contacted Falbrough?'

'The lines are dead; I expect there's a tree down somewhere. I tried to send a message, but Potts from the garage has taken somebody to Derling, and I just missed him. Then I went to Doctor Smythe, but he was on a call, and not expected back for hours. I didn't know who else to ask. There aren't that many car owners in the village and it's hardly the night to ask anyone to ride that far on a bike, the wind's so strong there's a chance they wouldn't make it.'

'Right, lad,' Deepbriar said. 'Here's what we do. I'll see if Major Brightman's willing to drive to Falbrough. You're to go home, get into some dry clothes as quick as you can, then get back to the Grigsdykes and start on house to house. Try Bridge Lane first, then work outwards from there. Ask everyone when they last saw Deirdre, or if they noticed any strangers about, and get them to look in sheds, outhouses, anywhere a child might have gone to hide, especially if it's somewhere she might get trapped. Once folk know the reason they won't mind being disturbed at this hour, most of them anyway. I'll join you as soon as I can.'

Once Giddens had gone, Deepbriar dashed upstairs, giving only a perfunctory knock at the bedroom door to warn the two women he was coming in.

'There's an emergency, and I have to go out,' he said.

The midwife looked scandalized at his sudden entrance. 'Thank you for letting us know, Mr Deepbriar,' she said frostily. 'Kindly leave the kettle filled on the back of the range in case I need it.'

Deepbriar nodded. He bent to kiss his wife's cheek; it was slightly damp with sweat, and he saw a change in her expression as a spasm of pain hit her.

'Don't worry about me,' she said, trying to smile. 'Go on, off you go.'

He obeyed, glad to be leaving what had become alien territory, but not without a touch of panic; there would be nobody in the house to fetch help if it was needed, and with the phone lines down and the doctor gone, where could they turn if anything went wrong? Back downstairs he put on his cape and pulled a sou'wester firmly down on his head, fastening it under his chin, before hurrying outside to retrieve his bike from the shed.

Deepbriar turned into the wind, battling against the driving rain and making the best speed he could; out in the open the gale was so strong that it was hard to draw any air into his lungs. Lightning flashed in the distance; there was another storm approaching across the moors. Thankfully it wasn't far to the

Brightmans' estate, and once he turned in at the gates, the avenue of trees along the drive to Minecliff Manor gave him a little shelter. There were still lights on downstairs, but it was a surprised Charles Brightman who came to the door, with Elaine not far behind; Mrs Brant, the housekeeper, must already have gone to bed.

'Thorny.' The major ushered his friend inside. 'Is something wrong? Can we help?'

Quickly Deepbriar explained about the missing child and the dead telephone lines. 'I don't like to ask you, not at this hour, but we're going to need help from Falbrough, and I can't see any other way of getting it.'

'I'll just fetch my coat,' Charles said, turning towards the back of the house. 'I'll take the Humber, and give you a lift back to Bridge Lane. Go and put your bike on board.'

Deepbriar opened the door, but Elaine stopped him. 'How's Mary?' she asked, 'I'm sorry I gave you a fright earlier.'

'It wasn't your fault. But I'm none too happy, to tell you the truth. The midwife's there, but nobody else. I'd like to fetch Mary's sister, but I don't think it's fair to ask. Her husband's working, and she couldn't leave the children alone, so she'd have to find somebody to stay with them, and there's no knowing when she'd be home.'

'Why don't I go?' Elaine offered. 'Charles

can drop me off on the way as well, and I'm happy to stay as long as I'm needed.'

'I think Mary would feel happier with you there,' Deepbriar said. 'The midwife's all very well, but it's not like having a friend in the house.'

There were far more lights on in Minecliff than was usual at eleven o'clock at night; as always, bad news had travelled fast, and there were little knots of men and women gathered in doorways, peering out into the storm.

Major Brightman drew up to let Deepbriar out of the Humber. As the constable removed his bike from the back of the car, several people braved the wind and rain to approach, some offering help, others more interested in gossip. It would be hard to conduct a satisfactory search in these conditions, but if Deirdre was still in Minecliff then the sooner they found her the better. If, God forbid, she had been spirited away like Janey Smithers, then speed was even more essential. Deepbriar told potential volunteers to gather at the village hall, though not before they had checked that the little girl wasn't hidden in one of their own homes. He assured them that either he or Constable Giddens would be along shortly, to tell them what to do.

Miss Cannon appeared at his side. 'I'll gather some of the WI,' she said. 'Anyone going out on a night like this will need hot tea and soup when they get back.'

Deepbriar found Constable Giddens a few doors from the Grigsdykes' house, a sodden notebook in his hand. 'Little boy here saw a black car driving down the road when he was on his way back to school at half past one,' he said. 'It doesn't look good, Thorny.'

'No, but we'd be unwise to make assumptions. We'll go on searching the village.' Deepbriar explained about the volunteers, and suggested where they might most usefully be employed. 'If you'll see to that, I'll carry on where you left off.'

Lightning and thunder exploded almost instantaneously over their heads, and both men ducked involuntarily. 'Shouldn't we start looking beyond Minecliff?' Giddens asked. 'Suppose she's on the moors? It's a terrible night for anyone to be out.'

'We don't have the manpower. Anyway, it's almost impossible to search open country at night in these conditions. We just have to pray she's in shelter somewhere.' Deepbriar didn't state the obvious; the child could be hundreds of miles away by now, if she'd been taken by car.

It was nearly one o'clock in the morning before the reinforcements from Falbrough arrived. Three men accompanied Major Brightman in the Humber, with four more travelling in a police car.

'There was a tree down, a mile out of town,' Charles explained, shouting over the noise of the storm, which had hardly abated. 'We rousted out the owner of the hardware shop and borrowed axes and saws to cut our way through. Luckily a couple of locals turned out to give us a hand, and we left them to finish the job.'

A uniformed sergeant was now the senior officer, but he didn't seem eager to take charge. 'Inspector Young's on his way. Until he gets here we'll just carry on with what you've got organized, Thorny. There's no point changing things every few minutes.'

'We think we've covered the village pretty thoroughly,' Deepbriar said. 'We were just gathering the volunteers in the village hall for a hot drink and a break, while we decided what to do next.'

'Any news from home?' Charles asked.

Deepbriar shook his head, resisting the temptation to look towards Stellings Lane.

'In that case I'll go and let Elaine know I'm back,' his friend said. 'Shan't be long.'

He returned a few minutes later to assure Deepbriar that all was proceeding as it should; Mary sent her love. The night wore on, with rain driven on the gusty wind, and a darkness so complete that a man could lose his way within yards of home. Inspector Young arrived to take charge, and the hunt for Deirdre went on into the early hours.

Men delved into sheds, poked around in overgrown gardens and shouted until they were hoarse. Eventually the obvious futility of the exercise drove both police and volunteers to seek shelter and wait for the dawn.

Deepbriar returned briefly to Stellings Lane, but there was still no news for him; Elaine was with Mary, and came on to the landing, a calm and competent presence. She spoke to him soothingly, as one might to a nervous child, promising to stay until the baby was born. Deepbriar stood in the kitchen for a few minutes, staring unseeingly at the range, listening to the faint hiss of the kettle. He couldn't bear to be indoors, so he took a torch and splashed along the footpaths threading the village, the mud almost to his knees; anything was better than pacing the floor.

As dawn approached the weather relented. Deepbriar checked in with Inspector Young, who told him to go home. Reluctantly, the constable obeyed. Inexpressibly weary, he closed the front door behind him, shutting out the noise of water running down the street and dripping from overflowing gutters. A different sound reached his ears. He set a hand on the newel post and listened; it was the unmistakable cry of a newborn baby. His heart in his mouth, he began to climb the stairs. Elaine opened the bedroom door and beamed down at him. Deepbriar felt the heavy weight that had oppressed him throughout the night being lifted from his shoulders.

'You're the father of a wonderful little girl,' Elaine said. 'But I think you'd better take off those clothes before you come in, or you may drown the poor child.'

Thorny Deepbriar spent the next few hours in a kind of daze, relieved to know that Mary had come through her ordeal so well. He had seen his daughter, crumpled of face, red and wrinkled, and declared her beautiful, as he knew he must; he was almost too tired to know what he was saying or doing. Now and then the image of the tiny white-wrapped bundle he'd held in his arms would appear in the back of his mind, but it was like a mirage conjured by his exhaustion. Nobody seemed to notice the state he was in; by mid-morning he was just one amongst the dozens of police officers who were involved in the hunt for Deirdre Grigsdyke.

Chief Inspector Stubbs had taken over from Inspector Young; several witnesses had confirmed that an unfamiliar car had been seen in the village at about the time Deirdre vanished.

'We seem to have eliminated all the usual callers,' Stubbs said, running a hand over the back of his neck. For the time being, Deepbriar had been ordered to stay at the village hall to help him, in case his local knowledge was needed. 'It wasn't the insurance agent, or the doctor from Derling who sometimes takes a call when the local man is busy.'

'And nobody had any visitors...' Deepbriar began, his eyes on the map that somebody had unrolled on the table.

'Sir, I think I have something.' A constable came hurrying in, followed by Kenny Rathbone, a railway signalman who lived in Bridge Lane, only five doors from the Grigsdykes' house. 'Mr Rathbone came home from work an hour ago, so he's only just heard about what's been happening. He tells me when he rode off on his bike yesterday he saw the car we're looking for, and the driver.'

'I was a bit surprised, Thorny,' Kenny said, 'I never knew Mr Lofthouse had a car, but I'm sure it was him.'

'Mr Lofthouse? The next-door neighbour?' Stubbs looked at Deepbriar. 'Does he own a car?'

Deepbriar shook his head. 'No. I didn't even know he could drive.'

'Is it likely he's bought one recently?'

'I doubt it.' Deepbriar rubbed his aching eyes. 'I can't believe he has anything to do with Deirdre's disappearance. He's a retired headmaster, and seventy years old if he's a day. He's very well thought of.' He noticed Rathbone listening with obvious interest. 'Anything else you can tell us, Kenny?' he asked. 'If not, you'll want to get home to your bed.'

With evident reluctance the man went. Stubbs dismissed the constable who had brought the railwayman in and turned to Deepbriar. 'We have to follow this up, if only to eliminate Lofthouse from our enquiries, no matter how spotless his reputation may be. If he wasn't home when the hunt for Deirdre began, presumably his house hasn't been searched.'

'He lives with his sister, sir. She must have been one of the first people Constable Giddens spoke to last night.'

Stubbs nodded. 'You and I had better go and have a word with her. Presumably she'll be able to tell us how her brother got hold of a car, and where the heck he's gone.'

'Sir?' Deepbriar grabbed his superior's sleeve as he reached the door, something he would never have done if he'd been wide awake and functioning properly. 'Miss Lofthouse is a bit fragile. I mean, she's—'

'She's what? Spit it out man,' Stubbs said impatiently.

Deepbriar did his best to put his thoughts in order. 'It's just that she's led a very sheltered life, and I suppose you might say she was simple. If her parents and her brother hadn't taken such good care of her she could have ended up in an institution. She keeps house, shops and cooks and so on, but she doesn't have much idea about what goes on outside her own little world. I'm not sure how she'll take to a couple of large policemen wanting to ask her questions.'

'Are you saying you want to interview her on your own?'

Deepbriar shook his head. 'No, sir, but perhaps I could do the talking. At least my face is familiar to her.'

'As long as she tells us what we want to know, I don't see any harm in that,' Stubbs replied, 'but don't waste time pussyfooting around, Deepbriar, we need answers.'

Miss Lofthouse answered the constable's knock quickly, her pale eyes blinking as if the light was too bright. She gave Deepbriar a smile, but looked a little nervous at the sight of Chief Inspector Stubbs.

'Hello, Miss Lofthouse,' Deepbriar said. 'I wonder if we could come in for a chat? You'll have heard about Deirdre Grigsdkye going missing. This is a colleague of mine, Chief Inspector Stubbs, he's in charge of the search for her.'

'I don't usually invite anybody in when my brother's not here,' Miss Lofthouse said uncertainly.

'It's a bit cold with the door open though, isn't it?' Deepbriar suggested. 'This won't take long, we're visiting everybody in the village. We would have liked to see Mr Lofthouse. It's a shame he isn't here.'

'Oh yes, it is,' she replied, standing back to let them in. 'I always miss him when he goes away. Please wipe your feet, I like to keep things spick and span for Edward.'

'I can see you do a good job,' Deepbriar said, removing his hat as he stepped over the threshold. 'Where has Mr Lofthouse gone?'

'Off on one of his little holidays. I don't know exactly where; he never books any accommodation until he arrives in Cumberland. He doesn't care for big hotels, you see; he prefers to stay at a farm, or a private guest house. Poor Edward, he used to be a very accomplished climber at one time, but his health is not so good now. He still loves climbing mountains, but he keeps to the easier paths.'

'It's not the ideal weather for walking,' Stubbs put in.

Miss Lofthouse looked a little startled at the interruption, staring at Deepbriar as if she suspected him of somehow saying these words without opening his mouth.

The constable hurried on. 'Did Mr Lofthouse take the bus into Cawster to catch the train?' he asked.

'No, he borrowed a motor car from his friend, Mr Addison. Such a dear boy. Mr Addison was Edward's pupil, you see, many years ago. He's grown up now of course, but we still see him from time to time. It all worked out so nicely, because he's deputy headmaster at my brother's old school, and he doesn't use his car much during the term.'

'I don't remember ever seeing Mr Lofthouse driving a car.'

'No, usually Edward goes to the school to collect it, but Mr Addison was visiting Falbrough, so he came here on his way; he has a particular interest in old churches.' She beamed. 'St Michael's is especially lovely, don't you think?'

'So they went off in the car together?' Stubbs asked.

'No,' Miss Lofthouse replied. 'Edward wasn't quite ready to leave. Mr Addison stopped for a quick cup of tea and then caught the bus. He'd do anything for my brother, he's devoted to him, like so many of his old pupils.' Miss Lofthouse frowned suddenly. 'Dear me, I've been running on a little, haven't I? Why do you want to know all these things?'

'Because young Deirdre from next door is missing,' Deepbriar reminded her. 'We're trying to find anybody who might have seen her since yesterday lunchtime, after about half past one. We think that might include Mr Lofthouse, and presumably this friend of his as well.'

'Oh no, not Mr Addison. He caught the mid-morning bus,' Miss Lofthouse said decidedly. 'I doubt if my brother saw her either, I didn't. I stood at the gate and waved

197

when he drove away,' she added.

'Well, because we still haven't found Deirdre we have to check on every possibility,' Deepbriar said. 'Suppose she'd managed to hide herself in the boot of the car?'

'Why would she do a thing like that?' Miss Lofthouse asked, smiling. 'That would be silly.'

'You don't seem very worried about her,' Chief Inspector Stubbs put in, unable to keep silent any longer.

Once again the elderly woman seemed surprised to find him there. 'Oh.' She thought for a moment, before shaking her head. 'She's a very sensible little girl.' Miss Lofthouse looked appealingly at Deepbriar. 'Should I be worried?'

'No, probably not,' he replied, keeping his eyes carefully averted from his superior and making a move to leave. 'Thank you for talking to us, Miss Lofthouse. We won't bother you any further for the moment.'

'It's been no bother,' she said, following them to the door. 'Please call again.'

'I see what you meant,' Stubbs said heavily, once they were outside and the door was closed. 'Next best thing to cloud-cuckoo-land.'

'She's not that bad, sir,' Deepbriar protested. 'She gave us what we need; it won't be hard to trace Mr Addison.'

'But her brother's off walking up mountains somewhere. A bit odd that, at this time of year. Suppose this Lofthouse is the pervert we've been looking for all along?'

Chapter Thirteen

'Edward Lofthouse is far too old to be the man who accosted June Day,' Deepbriar said, as he and the chief inspector walked back to the police house.

'I accept that, but he has to be questioned, if only to eliminate him from our enquiries.' Stubbs looked at Deepbriar with something like sympathy. 'Are you feeling all right, Thorny? When did you last have any sleep?'

'I'm fine, sir.' Deepbriar lied. There was a buzzing in his head, as if a swarm of bees was circling between his ears. If he didn't lie down soon he thought he might fall down, but the trouble was, he liked Mr Lofthouse, and his sister; he had to do his best to protect them from the malicious gossip that was bound to follow any police investigation. If the police in Cumberland were alerted, with an enquiry about the disappearance of a child, their search for Lofthouse could become headline news. Mud had a tendency to stick. Even if, as Deepbriar suspected, Lofthouse was proved to be as pure as the driven snow, there would be talk.

Deepbriar did his best to voice his concerns to Stubbs, making much of the fact that the school where Lofthouse had been headmaster might suffer too; it was very well known and much respected. The local gentry sent their sons there, but the board was generous with scholarships for bright children from less wealthy backgrounds.

The chief inspector sighed. 'I don't know what you expect me to do, Deepbriar. If I had the manpower I might send somebody to Cumberland, but we're already stretched to the limits. You know as well as I do, every lead has to be followed up. We can't ignore this.'

'Perhaps we could contact Mr Addison at the school, and see if his story tallies.' A sudden thought made its way through the fog in his brain. 'There's just a chance Mr Lofthouse might have told him where he planned to stay.'

'I suppose that won't hurt, but we need somebody to talk to Lofthouse soon, and since we don't know exactly where to find him, the police up in Cumberland are our best bet.' Stubbs pushed open the door of the police house, went into the empty office and picked up the telephone receiver. He tapped the instrument several times, before putting the receiver back on its cradle with more force than was necessary. Obviously the lines hadn't yet been repaired.

The chief inspector turned to Deepbriar, looking irritated. 'Doesn't look as if we'll be talking to anybody just yet. If you want to stop me digging into Mr Lofthouse's past, then tell me where to find this little girl. As far as we know, no other cars were seen in or around Minecliff at the relevant time.'

'So this time we're pretty sure we're not looking for an old Daimler,' Deepbriar said.

'No, whatever happened to Deirdre Grigsdyke, it's unlikely she was spirited away by the man who attacked June Day, unless he's changed his car.'

'No, sir,' Deepbriar said dispiritedly. There was an annoying ringing in his ears. He couldn't recall ever feeling so tired, yet he had an idea that when he did eventually get into bed, he wouldn't be able to sleep.

Stubbs made an impatient sound in his throat. 'Right now you're to go home for a few hours' rest, Constable. Get some sleep. That's an order.' He turned on his heel and strode out.

Deepbriar stood bemused for a few minutes, wondering what to do. Sleep had become beyond him somehow, a forgotten skill, but he had been given a direct order, and it was one he must obey. At least, he would go home. So far he had only seen his baby daughter for a few moments. Mary was very forgiving about the demands of his job, but she must be feeling neglected. A normal father would be showering his wife with attention, not to mention a bouquet of flowers, though that wouldn't be easy at this

time of year. The thought brought Deepbriar's thoughts back to Lavinia Lofthouse;
she had a greenhouse, and was renowned for
the cut flowers she produced for the church.
He would go to Bridge House again, and
talk to her without Stubbs breathing down
his neck; needing a bunch of flowers for his
wife would give him the perfect excuse.

'How nice,' Miss Lofthouse said, opening
the door much more willingly than on the
previous occasion. 'What can I do for you,
Constable?'

He explained about Mary and his daughter, and the old lady was immediately
enchanted to hear about the arrival of a new
baby. 'I have the very thing,' she said, leading
him out through the back door and into the
garden. The greenhouse was full of exotic
blooms, none of which he could name, and
she picked a large bunch, expertly arranging
them, then taking them indoors to finish the
whole thing off with tissue paper and ribbon.

'Miss Lofthouse, that's magnificent,'
Deepbriar said sincerely. 'I don't suppose
you'll allow me to pay for them, but perhaps
you'd accept a donation for the church. It
looks as if I've deprived the rector of next
week's display.'

'You may put a little extra in the plate on
Sunday,' the woman said happily. 'Give Mrs
Deepbriar my congratulations. I shall call in
a week or two, when she is up and about.'

'I'll do that, and thank you again.' Deep-briar paused in the hall, looking at the photographs that covered the walls in the hall. 'Mr Lofthouse has been on a lot of these climbing expeditions, hasn't he?'

'Oh yes, he's visited some wonderful places.' She pointed. 'That one was taken in the Alps, and the one below is in the Andes.'

'But didn't he have a nasty accident one time? Six years ago, wasn't it? I seem to remember he came out of hospital just in time for Christmas,' Deepbriar said.

'Oh my, you do have a good memory.' She scanned the photographs and indicated one in the top row. 'He was in Scotland with a group from the school. A boy got into diffi-culty, and Edward and another man went to help him. They say that but for Edward, the boy might have fallen to his death. He was saved, but my poor brother was badly hurt. That was the last time he was able to cope with the really difficult climbs, and he was in hospital for months, it was all very trying. Mr Addison said he should have had an award for bravery, but Edward hated the idea, so his friends and colleagues didn't pursue the matter.'

Deepbriar peered at the caption below the photograph. It was dated the end of Sep-tember 1951, three weeks before Miriam Pitt was abducted.

'That picture was taken the day before he

had his fall,' Miss Lofthouse said sadly.

'At least he can still enjoy walking,' Deepbriar said. 'I'm surprised he doesn't let you know where he's staying, just in case you need him for any reason.'

'Oh, didn't I tell you about our little arrangement? I'm sorry, I am becoming quite forgetful. He calls me on the telephone, as soon as he finds a telephone box near to his accommodation. I expect to hear from him very shortly.'

'The telephone lines came down in last night's storm,' Deepbriar said, 'so he might not be able to get through.'

'Oh dear. Well, perhaps they'll soon be mended.' She gave him a bright smile and opened the door. 'Thank you so much for calling, Constable. Do come again.'

There was still nobody in the office at the police house, so Deepbriar left a note for Chief Inspector Stubbs, explaining about Edward Lofthouse's accident, which cleared him of any possible involvement in the case of Miriam Pitt. He added that his sister should know the man's whereabouts as soon as the telephone service was restored.

Deepbriar made his way home to Stellings Lane, glad there weren't many people about. He was very conscious of the huge bouquet he was carrying; he might not be Minecliff's local bobby any more, but there was still a certain dignity involved in being a police officer, and he knew it to be a fragile thing, especially among the less respectable members of the community.

Mary was propped up in bed, looking very pretty in her best bed-jacket. Only Aggie was there, which was a relief, and she was unusually considerate, vanishing downstairs as soon as Deepbriar came in, saying she would make him tea and a sandwich.

'You look terribly tired,' Mary said, as Deepbriar bent to look at the tiny new arrival in the crib beside their bed. 'Have you had any sleep?'

'Been too busy,' he said, giving his wife a kiss and bringing the flowers out from behind his back. 'For you,' he added lamely. To his consternation she burst into tears. He stood aghast, until he realized she was laughing at the same time.

'Oh Thorny, how lovely!' she said, once she could catch her breath. 'You've not had a moment to spare, you come in here with a two-day beard and smelling like a cow byre, but you bring me the most beautiful flowers!'

He sat beside her then, and put his arm around her. 'I haven't even asked how you feel,' he said.

'Tired, but very happy,' she replied. 'Isn't she wonderful?'

'Nearly as lovely as her mother,' Deepbriar said. 'What do you want to call her? I always liked the name Rose, but not with Deep-briar.'

'There are other pretty flowers. Violet, Primrose, Poppy....'

'I like Poppy.' He got up to look at the baby again, still amazed at how tiny she was. She looked as if she could nestle quite comfortably on one of his hands. 'What do you think, little 'un, do you fancy Poppy?' The baby's tiny mouth opened and closed briefly, as if in unconscious acknowledgement.

'Poppy Rose,' Mary said decidedly. 'And now, you'd better go, Thorny.'

'Oh, sorry. I expect you need some rest,' he said, backing towards the door.

'Not as much as you do,' she replied serenely. 'I asked Aggie to put a pillow and some blankets in the living room, you won't be disturbed there, though the sofa's a bit small.'

'I could sleep on a bed of nails right now and not notice,' he replied, blowing her a kiss. 'G'night, love.'

'It's barely midday,' she protested, smiling, but he'd already gone.

He was striding across the open moor, rain battering him. Suddenly a large metal box stood in his way, and he recognized it as the safe from Fielders, the one with the complicated time mechanism. In the illogic of his dream, he knew he must get it open. The metal rings with their inscribed numbers were suddenly huge, and beside them were the hands of a clock, spinning round wildly. Panic struck him; he must get the safe open. Deirdre was inside, he was sure of it, and if he didn't rescue her then she would suffocate.

Deepbriar racked his brain for a sequence of numbers that would open the door, and as his weary brain struggled with the problem, figures began appearing, like sums in an arithmetic book, while others crawled across a page of a telephone directory. Things were becoming more and more surreal, a gigantic row of numbers peeling off the paper and beginning to dance around him. As if speaking close to his ear, a voice said; *'It's not just phone numbers, I've got a very bad memory.'* A gigantic figure nine began to wrap itself around Deepbriar's legs. With a yelp he tried to kick it away, coming abruptly awake as he fell off the sofa with the blanket tangled around his feet.

The afternoon was fading into night. Deepbriar stared between the ill-fitting curtains at the darkening sky; his dream had provided him with an answer. He knew why Fielders hadn't been searched as thoroughly as any of the other factories, and he knew exactly what the eccentric thief was up to. There was something he must do, right now, if he was to prevent a much more serious crime.

There wasn't really time to shave, but he

couldn't go outside looking like a tramp, even in an emergency. He ran to the kitchen, relieved to find the kettle was hot; obviously Aggie was still around somewhere. The wash and shave were rushed; he resented the time it took to go upstairs to find a clean shirt, and he dragged his dirty clothes back on, wrinkling his nose at his muddy trouser turn-ups. Deepbriar hurried to the police house, breathing a sigh of relief when he saw that the car that had brought Chief Inspector Stubbs was still there. He ran his boss to ground in the village hall.

'Sir, the petty-cash thefts. I've worked it out,' he said breathlessly. 'I know why that blighter's been breaking in to all those factories. I'm sorry, I know that with little Deirdre missing you won't want to worry about this right now, but I think we'll need to act quickly, in case he's finally got what he wanted.'

Stubbs listened attentively as Deepbriar explained his theory, nodding now and then but not interrupting once. 'It all sounds very plausible,' he said, as the constable finished. He looked at his watch. 'There's no real reason to suppose it will happen this week.'

'No, sir. But only two firms are at risk tonight. I think we ought to warn them, and maybe alert the beat bobbies in those areas.'

Stubbs nodded. 'I think we can do more than that; it's worth a gamble if we've a chance of catching this villain. I'm tired of being made to look a fool. We'll ask uniform to spare us a couple of men.' He gave Deepbriar a searching look. 'Are you fit for duty, Constable?'

'Yes, sir, I've had a meal and some sleep. I'm sorry if I still look rather scruffy, I shaved in a bit of a rush, but if he does strike tonight we've only got a couple of hours to set everything up. Time's a bit tight, to say the least of it.'

'There's one thing in our favour,' Stubbs said, reaching for the telephone. 'The lines have been repaired, so I can call ahead and tell Sergeant Jakes to expect you, and get the uniformed men organized. Go home, tidy yourself up and get back here in fifteen minutes. I'll find somebody to drive you to the station. I only wish I could come too, but it looks as if it should be a clear night, so we'll go on searching.'

'You're sure you want me to go, sir?' Deepbriar asked. He glanced across the room; Peg and Alf Grigsdyke were standing together by the door. The expression on their faces wrenched at his heart, newly softened by the arrival of his daughter.

'Half the men in the village have volunteered to keep helping,' Stubbs replied, 'so shortage of local knowledge isn't a problem. We've also had an offer from the TA. I gather they have a detachment standing by;

one or two men here or there won't make much difference.' The chief inspector smiled wearily. 'If you're right, then there's a chance you could be about to crack your very first solo case, DC Deepbriar. You've got a knack for bringing us good luck, and the Lord knows we could do with some.'

Deepbriar wriggled his toes inside his boots, trying to keep the circulation going. The water they were standing in was only half an inch deep, but the temperature had dropped several degrees since they arrived. 'We'll be frozen solid at this rate,' he grumbled. 'I don't know how we're expected to run after this villain if our feet are stuck in a block of ice.'

'I looked all round, but this was the only place where we could get a clear view of the wall but still stay out of sight,' PC Harry Bartle said, his breath turning to icy mist as he spoke. 'You really think this thief is going to come back to Corders and try again?'

Deepbriar stared at the factory's perimeter wall. 'Maybe not tonight, but he'll return to the scene of one of the break-ins soon, I'm sure of it. All he's been doing up to now is what Mitch O'Hara would call *casing the joint*.'

'But he broke in!'

'Yes, and after he'd had a good scout round and found what he was looking for, he left, pretty much empty handed. Unless we accepted Sergeant Jakes's theory that the silly beggar was crazy, there had to be a logical explanation for what he was doing. Luckily he acted differently when he raided Fielders, and that was what gave me the clue.'

'What do you mean?'

'At Fielders it was obvious he hadn't made such a diligent search. There were small items he could easily have stolen, but he didn't. I doubt if he did much more than locate the cash-box, glance round the office, then push off home.'

Bartle shook his head. 'I don't get it.'

'The whole point of the robberies was to find out how to steal the money that was brought in to pay the wages. One look at Fielders' safe told him he'd be wasting his time there. Luckily for him, there were other places where he discovered everything he needed to know, like when the money arrived, when it was paid out, and, most important, whether he could open the safe.'

'So he'll be breaking into the safe here, if he comes tonight? You mean he's a cracksman? Do you think he'll be using dynamite?' The constable's eyes looked wide in the darkness.

Deepbriar smiled at the youngster's expression. 'There won't be any need for dynamite. People take a lot for granted. They don't realize it's not a good idea to write down the combination to a safe, if they have trouble remembering it, or to hide a key in a cupboard, rather than entrust it to a member of staff.'

There was a silence as Harry Bartle digested what he'd heard. Deepbriar meanwhile was beginning to have doubts. There was a very good chance he'd got it wrong; they could wait here all night, and outside the other factories tomorrow, and absolutely nothing would happen. Depression was looming when Harry spoke again, bringing him out of his gloomy reverie.

'Mr Deepbriar?' the young constable said tentatively.

'Call me Thorny,' Deepbriar reminded him. 'What?'

'I can't help thinking about Deirdre Grigsdyke. If she'd been out on the moor, wouldn't she have been found by now? Only it's so cold.'

Deepbriar grimaced. 'She's a country girl and she's not a fool. If she left home voluntarily I think she'd have the sense to go where there's a bit of shelter. Chief Inspector Stubbs is sure somebody grabbed her, even though it looks as if that car's a red herring.'

Young Harry shook his head. 'I've been thinking about that. This isn't really like the Janey Smithers case. Somehow, I doubt if this is the first time Deirdre's made herself scarce. You know what Alf's like when he's had a few. Maybe she ran away.'

'I did think about it, but Alf's usually broke by midweek. It would be different if she'd gone off on a Friday or Saturday night.'

'Ah, but this particular Wednesday there was a darts tournament. Alf's a dab hand with the arrows, I've seen him get his team out of a fix quite a few times, and when he does, every other man buys him a pint.'

Deepbriar stared at his companion; as the son of the publican at the Speckled Goose, Harry would know about such things. 'You really think Deirdre's run off? But where would she go? She's got plenty of friends and relations, and I suppose any one of them might take her in for a night, but they'd have let Peg know where she was.'

'Perhaps she doesn't want to be found,' Harry suggested. 'They're still searching the old airfield; you know what a maze that is. I heard the chief inspector talking about using dogs, to see if they can pick up her scent.'

'After all that rain?' Deepbriar sniffed, as if testing the air himself. 'Not a hope.'

The walkie-talkie that Deepbriar had secreted under his coat squawked into life. Sergeant Jakes's voice came on air. He sounded breathless, as if he'd been running.

'A man just climbed in over the wall, Thorny. God knows how, but it looks as if you've got it right. You'd better get over here, we might need reinforcements. Send Bartle

214

to the front entrance, and you join me where we agreed, at the corner on the north-eastern side.'

Deepbriar acknowledged the order. 'You heard the man,' he said, 'let's go.' Jakes and Reed had staked out the tyre factory, the only other place where the payroll was stored in the safe on a Thursday night.

As he and Bartle headed back to their bikes, Deepbriar grinned to himself. Jakes had been dismissive of his plan to use bicycles, but by taking a short cut by the canal and through the park, they could cover the distance to the factory much more quickly than a man in a car.

Chapter Fourteen

Deepbriar's heart was pounding; he was putting every ounce of effort into keeping up with Harry Bartle, but still the younger man was drawing ahead. He felt a guilty thrill as they sped through the park; they were breaking the bylaws, not merely cycling but racing headlong between the flower-beds and along the rose-walk. Ahead of them, gleaming darkly in a fleeting ray of moonshine, lay the lake; skirt around that and they were almost there.

Harry looked back. 'All right if I go on?' he called.

'Good idea,' Deepbriar gasped, 'but keep out of sight. He's no fool and we don't want him giving us the slip.' Harry nodded, skidding out into the road with grit spurting from beneath his wheels.

In another two minutes Deepbriar was crouched at Sergeant Jakes's side in the shadows behind the factory wall, his breath wheezing from aching lungs, and his leg muscles feeling like jelly.

'You wouldn't be out of breath if you'd come by car,' Jakes said.

'If I'd come by car I wouldn't be here yet,'

Deepbriar gasped, 'and young Bartle was well ahead of me.'

Jakes shifted restlessly. 'Our man's been quite a while. I hope we haven't missed him. He went up that tree like a monkey, jumped across to the wall and vanished.' Jakes sounded worried. 'Somebody that good at climbing could get out through a window on the far side and be gone before we know it. I wish we had more men.'

'I'll go round there,' Deepbriar offered.

'No, I'll go. Stay here and get your breath back.' Jakes grinned in the darkness as he rose to his feet. 'You won't mind if I take your bike? It's been a while, but they say you never forget.'

Minutes dragged by. Deepbriar stared along the factory wall until there were bright lights popping in front of his eyes. The silence was broken by the sound of running footsteps pounding along the road; Constable Reed was racing towards him.

'He's gone,' Reed gasped. 'I was too far away to do anything. He can't have known I was there, but he was taking no chances; he came out over the wall, sprinted across the road and climbed into Hoskin's yard. I followed, but I lost him. The place was quiet as the grave.'

'He'll have run through the railway sidings,' Deepbriar said. 'He knows the area, that's for sure.'

Reed nodded. 'I called Sergeant Jakes on the walkie-talkie, and he said he'd meet us back here.'

A few minutes later the four officers stood in a disconsolate huddle. 'Now what?' Jakes said, 'Stubbs will roast us!'

'There's still a chance,' Deepbriar said suddenly. 'He's a cheeky beggar. While we're standing here he could be on his way to Corders.' He took the bike from Jakes's passive grip and jerked his head at Bartle, a grin on his face. 'Come on, Harry, we'll give 'em a race.'

Jakes and Reed ran off to the police car they'd left hidden in the next street, while the two cyclists tore back towards the park. 'Suppose he doesn't go in where we expected?' Harry asked, keeping his speed down to stay alongside Deepbriar.

'There aren't so many options at Corders,' Deepbriar replied. 'You go to that stretch of wall where we were keeping watch, and I'll take the turning into the main road. The car will be coming from the other direction, so between us we should have all his escape routes covered. Go on, lad, don't wait for me. But don't go getting yourself into trouble either,' he called at the young man's back, the gap between them already widening.

Deepbriar could feel his pulse pounding in his head, in his neck, and right down to his hands and feet, but he wasn't going to slow

218

down. He told himself that Harry would be fine, though since that hadn't been the case on either occasion when they'd collaborated on cases in the past, he wasn't hopeful. 'Third time lucky,' he muttered, vowing to get fitter. If he didn't, by the time little Poppy was old enough to run about in the garden he wouldn't be able to keep up with her. At last he turned out of the park. He swept round a bend; Corders was only a couple of hundred yards ahead.

The clouds shifted and a timely moonbeam shone down on to the scene. A man was lowering himself from the top of the wall, his outline strangely misshapen. As he reached the ground and straightened, Deepbriar could see that the man had a knapsack on his back.

A bicycle came tearing across the road. Harry Bartle executed a flamboyant dismount while still on the move, to come to an abrupt halt two yards in front of the startled thief.

'Evening, sir,' the young constable said. 'Nice night for it.'

Having stood frozen for maybe a second the crook started to his right, only to see Deepbriar approaching fast. He turned the other way, but as Harry put out a hand and laid it on the man's shoulder, the police car appeared at the far end of the street.

'Sorry, sir,' Constable Bartle said, failing

to suppress a grin. 'I should have made it clear straight away. You're surrounded. And you're under arrest.'

Sergeant Jakes bounded out of the car, with Reed a few steps behind him. He stopped short when he got a clear view of their captive's face. 'I know you,' he said.

'Don't tell me he's got a record,' Deepbriar groaned. 'I thought we'd checked all the local villains a dozen times.'

'No, this is Tony Norman. He's a postman, and before that he was a milkman. Obviously he got tired of working for a living.'

The prisoner flushed, his shoulders drooping. Jakes turned to Bartle. 'Right, since you made the arrest, Constable, you'd better fetch him along to the station with me. Constable Reed will bring your bike.'

It hardly seemed possible for Harry's smile to get any wider, yet somehow it did. He pointed out that Thorny had been the senior officer when the man was captured, but Jakes waved his protests away, ushering the constable and his captive to the patrol car. He gave Deepbriar a wink as he turned to follow. 'You'll be in charge once you get back,' he whispered, 'but let the lad enjoy his moment of glory, eh?'

Tony Norman wasn't reluctant to talk; in fact he seemed quite cheerful as he made his statement. 'I couldn't resist it, see,' he said at last, when all the formalities were over. 'Not once I figured out how easy it would be. Nobody takes much notice of a postman, they just see the uniform; I could hang around in offices having a chat for a few minutes, and the staff carried on as usual. Comptons have gone now, but that's where I got the idea. There was this woman, Mrs Goldby. She'd only been working in the office for a couple of weeks. When somebody asked her to open the safe, she picked up her handbag, and looked through a little notebook. It wasn't hard to guess why. That set me thinking. How many people find it hard to remember numbers? And what about the safes that need a key? There was one place where they locked the safe key in a little box on the wall, and you could have broken into that with a tin opener. I was willing to bet there were plenty of offices where the keys were left in a drawer, just waiting to be found.'

'But why didn't you break in when there was money in the safe?' Bartle asked.

'Because it could take time to locate the key, or the combination.' Norman leant forward, eager to tell the rest of his story. 'I decided to find two or three possible targets before I took anything, and go for one big haul. Of course, I couldn't completely hide the fact that I'd broken in, so I'd steal a few little bits and pieces, to make it look as if that's what I was after. While I was there I'd check when they took delivery of the wages, and when they paid them out.'

'I suppose you'd open the safe, just to make sure you could?' Deepbriar said.

'Yes. A bit of a laugh, that was. One time I was tempted, because somebody had left nearly thirty quid in the safe, but taking it would have spoilt the whole scheme.' The man sighed. 'I'd worked it out so carefully. You don't do a milk round for five years without getting to know what goes on around the town at night. I knew all the local beats, and there wasn't much risk of walking into a copper. I waited for a time when there was a flap on. Go to the right place for a drink after lunch and you can get all the latest gossip. I guessed you'd have all your men out looking for that little girl, it was no secret. Tonight should have been perfect.'

Bartle grinned. 'You reckoned without Falbrough's secret weapon. Sherlock Deepbriar, that's what they ought to call him.'

Thorny glowered at the youngster. 'That'll do,' he growled. 'All right, Norman, let's see you locked up for what's left of the night. We'll not be able to get you to court early in the morning; you'll have to cool your heels in the cells for a bit. We've still got a missing child to find.'

When he arrived home, some hours later, Deepbriar crept in as quietly as he could, but his care wasn't necessary, for Mary called to him as he closed the door. 'Come up, Thorny, we've hardly seen you.' She had Poppy to her breast. 'You're not going to be prudish about this, are you?' she asked, looking up. 'There's nothing more natural than a woman feeding a baby.'

'Of course not,' Deepbriar said gruffly, the beginnings of a lump in his throat. He would have liked to give voice to his feelings, but the words didn't come. The baby was a miracle so unexpected that he could still hardly comprehend his good fortune. If it hadn't been for Deirdre Grigsdyke he would have been perfectly happy at that moment. Determinedly putting the missing child to the back of his mind, he gave Mary a quick account of the night's events. She laughed aloud when he told her how Harry had made his arrest. 'Bless the boy,' she said. 'Phyllis and Don are so proud of him.'

'And so they should be. He's got the makings of a good copper.' Deepbriar yawned widely as Mary laid Poppy, now sound asleep, back in her crib. 'Anything I can get for you, love?' he asked.

She shook her head. 'No. How about you? Aggie left some cold gammon.'

'No, I'm fine. I'm afraid I might sleep the clock round, though. I'll be glad to get back to normal hours, so I can move back in here with you. If I'm not up and about when Aggie comes, will you ask her to knock on the door?'

'I suppose so, though you look as if a solid eight hours would do you the world of good.' She lifted her face as he bent to kiss her. 'Goodnight, Daddy,' she said.

'Sleep tight, Mummy,' he rejoined, tiptoeing past his daughter and back downstairs.

Daylight came far too soon. Still bleary-eyed, Deepbriar went to report at the police house, where he found Chief Inspector Stubbs sitting at the desk that had once been his.

'Congratulations, Thorny,' Stubbs said. 'I was right, you did bring us luck.'

'PC Bartle made the arrest,' Deepbriar pointed out.

Stubbs nodded. 'By chasing after the thief on his bike, yes; I heard. You did a good job between you, but that makes no difference to my views on CID men needing to be able to drive. You got lucky last night, but you and Bartle would have been caught flat-footed if our villain had driven off in a car. Jakes took a hell of a risk, not nabbing him at the tyre factory.' The chief inspector gave Deepbriar a penetrating look. 'I'm not sure I've heard all there is to be said about that, but never mind, at least we'll be able to lock this man Norman up for a good long while, with two serious crimes on his sheet, as well as all the petty theft.'

'Yes, I wonder if he's regretting not settling

for life as a postman,' Deepbriar said, suppressing a yawn. 'Maybe I should have done the same; at least they have regular hours.'

There was the sound of a car drawing up outside. Stubbs stood, gathering up a few papers from in front of him. 'That will be Chief Superintendent Murray, he's taking over here while I get back to the Janey Smithers enquiry. We're short-handed again. Inspector Young put his foot down a rabbit hole and sprained his ankle last night. He hopes to be back on duty this afternoon, but we have to see what the doctor says; he couldn't put any weight on his foot at all when I last spoke to him.'

'Anything more on Deirdre, sir?' Deepbriar asked quickly, knowing he'd get short shrift once the chief superintendent came in.

'No. And we're running out of places to search. By the way, I saw Mr Addison, the owner of the car.'

They could hear voices; evidently Murray had been intercepted by another officer. Deepbriar made the most of his opportunity. 'You went there yourself, sir?'

'Yes. You seemed so sure that Lofthouse was innocent, and what with that business of him being in hospital when Miriam Pitt was murdered, I thought I'd better.' He sighed. 'I have to say I've come to the same conclusion. Edward Lofthouse is about the last person on earth you'd suspect of abducting a child. Did you know he'd had a family?'

'No, he's never spoken much about his personal life. He's a private sort of man.'

'He was married for thirty years, and lost two sons in the war. In 1944 he and his wife took his sister Lavinia into their home. Evidently she'd never been quite right, and when her parents died it looked as if she'd have to go into an asylum, but her brother stepped in. According to Addison, her condition improved so much, that by the time Mrs Lofthouse took sick and died a couple of years later, Lavinia Lofthouse was capable of taking over the household chores for her brother.'

'And when he retired they moved together to Minecliff,' Deepbriar said.

'Yes. Lofthouse stayed in close contact with the school, hence the climbing expeditions. Addison confirmed what Miss Lofthouse told us about the accident; when he fell he was risking his neck to save a silly young lad who'd disobeyed orders, but he didn't think twice about going to the rescue.' Stubbs grimaced. 'There's only one thing that might have involved him in Deirdre's disappearance, and that's if the girl hid herself in the car. If that's what happened, Lord knows where she might be by now.'

Stubbs paused, listening, as if to check that his superior officer wasn't coming, then he beckoned for Deepbriar to follow him through the house and into the kitchen. Here he turned to the constable again. 'Deepbriar, you know these people. I gather Grigsdyke can be violent. Is there any chance that he lost his temper and killed his own daughter?'

Thorny shook his head. 'Not halfway through the day, sir, no. You're right about him having a violent streak, but it's only ever when he's drunk.'

'Did this happen often?' Stubbs asked. 'Do you think the child might have run away because she was frightened of him?'

'It's possible. In fact, Constable Bartle said as much to me last night, and I think he probably knows more about the Grigsdkye family than I do. Would you like me to go and have a word with Alf and Peg?'

'Yes, I think you'd better,' Stubbs said. As Murray's voice came to them suddenly louder, the chief inspector jerked a thumb at the back door. 'What are you waiting for, Thorny? Get out of here, while you've got a chance.'

Deepbriar sat in a sagging armchair and stared in disbelief at Peg and Alf Grigsdyke, huddled side by side on a tired-looking sofa. 'Three times?' he bellowed. Alf looked ready to crumble under the constable's angry gaze. 'Deirdre ran off three times, and you never told us.'

'She didn't exactly run away,' Peg said, re-gaining some of her old spirit. 'She only went to her grandma the first time, and I fetched her back. It wasn't even dark. Then a few weeks later she went to my sister's. Her Uncle Arthur brought her home.'

'And the third time?'

'She went to her friend in Possington, and spun them some tale about me being poorly. Deirdre persuaded them to let her stay the night. She'd left me a note,' she added defensively, 'it's not as if I didn't know where she'd gone.'

Deepbriar recalled what he'd heard from Harry Bartle. 'Were these all occasions when Alf was playing in darts matches?'

Peg looked at her husband, her lips clamped into a thin line of displeasure, and the man nodded miserably. 'I can't help it,' he whined. 'When we win the rest of the team buy me drinks. It's not my fault if I have a pint or two.'

'You could try saying no,' Deepbriar said furiously. He rose to his feet, looming over them. 'So, when you found Deirdre was missing again, you went to call on all your friends and relations before you called the police. I hope you realize how much trouble you're in.'

Tears began to flow silently down Peg's weather-worn cheeks, and Deepbriar felt slightly ashamed of his outburst. Lowering his voice, he went on more quietly. 'Is there anybody she might have gone to, some relation or friend further away that you haven't checked? Do you have family in Falbrough, or Cawster?'

Peg shook her head. 'Deirdre wouldn't go that far, not on her own. She doesn't like towns, and she's not used to crowds.'

'She's gone somewhere,' Deepbriar said bleakly. 'Stay here,' he added, 'I'll have to go and tell my boss what you've told me.'

As he left the house, Deepbriar wondered if Edward Lofthouse could have found the girl in his borrowed car once he arrived in Cumberland; he might have been trying to get in touch ever since. It was unlikely; Lofthouse would have turned round and brought her straight back. He moved on to another tack. If Deirdre was desperate to hide, to get out of her father's reach, but she no longer trusted her friends or relations to keep her secret, where might she go? He could think of no obvious answer.

Deepbriar had almost passed Bridge House when he noticed that none of the curtains had been drawn, although it had been light for over an hour; Miss Lofthouse was always meticulous about such things. It would only take a moment to check that she was all right.

Deepbriar knocked on the door. There was no answer. Deepbriar lifted the letter-

229

box and peered in. 'Miss Lofthouse? It's Constable Deepbriar. I need to talk to you again.' There was no response, but as he watched, he saw the kitchen door move, just a little. If the old lady had been taken ill during the night, she might not be dressed yet. He didn't have time to waste; there was one approach she would be unable to resist. 'The telephone wires have been repaired,' Deepbriar called. We're a bit worried about Mr Lofthouse. Have you heard from him?'

A long slow minute passed before the kitchen door opened. Miss Lofthouse approached slowly, as if uncertain on her feet. 'My brother hasn't telephoned me yet,' she said.

'Are you all right, Miss Lofthouse? Can you open the door? It's uncomfortable stooping like this to talk to you.'

She did as he asked, and stood back with a wave of her hand to invite him inside. 'What did you mean?' she asked anxiously. 'Why are you worried about Edward?'

'I didn't really mean we're worried, just that we'd like to be sure he's safe,' Deepbriar improvised. 'Some of those farms up in the mountains are a long way from a telephone box, aren't they?' He swept off his hat and put it on the hall table. 'Are you feeling poorly, Miss Lofthouse?'

Her appearance had changed greatly from their previous encounters; she was pale, her hair was untidy, and she seemed unwilling to meet his eyes. He noticed that the buttons on her cardigan had been fastened haphazardly, and the garment hung crookedly on her thin frame. This was a woman far removed from the calm and neat little old lady he had spoken to the day before. And then the answer struck him.

'You know where Deirdre is, don't you?' Deepbriar said. 'Is she here in the house?'

To his consternation the woman dropped her head into her hands and began to cry.

'Miss Lofthouse?' This reaction was so unexpected that Deepbriar felt fear dry his mouth. The woman collapsed on to the bottom stair, wailing inconsolably, her fingers pulling at the hem of her cardigan with such strength that a few threads began to work loose. He had told Chief Inspector Stubbs that she was simple, but obviously her grip upon reality was more feeble than he had guessed. Something had pushed her over the edge, and it was something to do with Deirdre. Deepbriar dropped to his knees beside her.

'Nobody is going to hold you to blame, Miss Lofthouse, but you have to tell me,' he said gently. 'What do you know about Deirdre? Is she hurt? Did she get shut in somewhere?'

The abject figure before him was shaking violently, and the wailing grew louder. Deep-

231

briar felt as if a clenched fist was twisting itself into his stomach. 'I think I'd better take a look around the house, Miss Lofthouse.'

She looked up wildly at this, and began shaking her head.

'It's all right,' he said, 'look, I wiped my feet. You just sit there, I shan't be long.' The ground floor didn't take long. Deepbriar climbed the stairs two at a time, and paused on the landing; he had never been upstairs in Bridge House before. He worked quickly and methodically through three bedrooms and a bathroom, checking every place that was large enough to hide a child of ten, dead or alive.

There were two doors left on this floor. He opened the first, and found himself in a large bedroom which was plainly the preserve of Edward Lofthouse. The retired headmaster slept in a single bed but the room felt cramped; the walls were lined with books, as if the shelves in his study downstairs had overflowed. It didn't take Deepbriar a moment to check beneath the bed and behind the curtains, but then he stopped short. At the foot of the bed stood a chest, a huge thing made of ancient oak, and banded with metal. The lid must be very heavy; if a child opened it and climbed in there to hide, the chest would be very difficult to open from the inside. Once shut, it would probably be airtight. Was this where

Miss Lofthouse had found a sight that had broken her uncertain hold on her sanity?

Sick at heart, Deepbriar took a grip on the lid.

Chapter Fifteen

Deepbriar heaved at the lid; it was every bit as weighty as he feared. Downstairs Miss Lofthouse continued her keening wail, and he steeled himself for what he might find.

The lid rose. An object slid out, flopping softly against Deepbriar's leg, and his fingers almost lost their grip. He stared down at the thing that had landed with a thud on the floor. It was an ancient copy of *The Times,* faded with age. The whole trunk was full of newspapers.

His hand shaking a little, Deepbriar closed the trunk, and satisfied himself that there was nowhere else in this room that could conceal the child. He returned to the corridor and pulled open the one remaining door. A flight of stairs vanished into darkness; he hadn't known that the house had an attic.

'Deirdre? Are you up there?' The words echoed in the stairwell. Spotting a light-switch on the wall, he flicked it on and began to climb. Somebody had been this way recently; the dust that lay thickly on the treads had been disturbed.

'I promised not to tell,' the wild wail from behind him made Deepbriar turn and look back. Miss Lofthouse was at the foot of the stairs, wringing her hands like a madwoman. 'Cross my heart and hope to die,' she cried frantically, dropping to her knees. 'You mustn't. You mustn't!'

'Please, Miss Lofthouse.' Deepbriar stood aghast as this apparition began to climb after him on her hands and knees. She looked nothing like the smiling woman who had sent him away with a bouquet for his wife only the day before.

'Calm down, Miss Lofthouse,' he said, hopelessly out of his depth in the face of her derangement. 'Stay where you are, please. You'll hurt yourself.'

She lifted her head to look up at him. 'You mustn't go up there. I promised.'

'Promised?' Deepbriar asked. 'Who made you promise? Was it your brother? You have to tell me, Miss Lofthouse.'

A key grated in a lock. Deepbriar whipped around, so quickly he almost lost his footing on the stairs. Above him, a door opened. Deirdre Grigsdyke appeared on the top step. Her hair was untidy, with a ribbon dangling forlornly below one ear. By the light of the bare bulb her face looked dark and shadowed, and as she started to come down towards him Deepbriar could see that it was swollen and wet with tears. But she was very much alive. He had never seen a sight more welcome.

He turned to look at Miss Lofthouse as she began to wail again. She had tipped back precariously to sit on her heels, shaking from head to toe. With her hands held tight over her eyes, the tears that were squeezing out between her fingers were running down her arms.

Deirdre dashed down, squeezing past Deepbriar to fling her arms around the old lady. Already insecure, Miss Lofthouse swayed and almost fell, but Deirdre moved quickly, turning her gently so she was able to sit on a step.

Deirdre sat down too, putting an arm round the old lady, and looking a lot like her mother as she glared up at Deepbriar. 'Leave her alone,' she said. 'She didn't do anything wrong.'

'I never said she did,' Deepbriar protested.

The child gave him what Mary would call an old-fashioned look, before turning to Miss Lofthouse and speaking softly in her ear. 'It's all right, you didn't break your promise,' she said. 'There's nothing to worry about.'

'Are you sure?' The old lady plucked nervously at the sleeve of Deirdre's jumper.

'Yes. Cross my heart and hope to die.' Deirdre looked up at the constable, and suddenly she was a vulnerable child once more. 'Please, tell her that she won't get into trouble. It was all my fault, not hers.'

'Neither of you has anything too serious to

worry about,' Deepbriar said. 'Why don't you go and put the kettle on, Miss Lofthouse? We could do with a cup of tea.'

The old lady looked up at him before glancing around, as if surprised to find herself sitting on the attic stairs. Gently, she removed herself from the child's grasp. 'That's a good idea.' She stood up, brushed dust off her skirt, tutted over the badly fastened cardigan and rebuttoned it correctly. With a vague smile she left the child and the constable looking slightly bemusedly at each other.

'Do I have to go home now?' There were unshed tears in Deirdre's eyes. 'Has my dad been shouting?'

'No, he's not done any shouting since you went missing. He and your mum have been frantic with worry. They thought something very bad might have happened to you.'

The girl's mouth turned down, her lips trembling. 'Something bad happens every time my dad plays darts. When he comes home he's not the same. He's not nice any more. And sometimes he frightens Mum and Willy.'

'That's why you came here?' Deepbriar said.

She nodded. 'I crept in the back door when Miss Lofthouse was saying goodbye to Mr Lofthouse. Nobody comes up to the attic much, and I knew she wouldn't, not when he's away. She only found me because I was hungry. I went to the kitchen to look for some breakfast before she got out of bed, but I dropped the butter dish.'

Deepbriar nodded. 'And you made her promise not to tell anybody.'

'Yes. Cross your heart and hope to die,' Deirdre said. 'I don't know why she got so upset. It doesn't really mean anything. Everyone says it at school, all the time.'

'It means something to a person like Miss Lofthouse. When I came to the door she was terrified. In some ways she's more of a child than you are.'

Deirdre looked down at her feet. 'Auntie Lavinia has always been nice to me, but she went a bit funny. I was scared, so I ran back up to the attic and shut myself in.'

'She was scared too.' He held out his hand. 'Now, it's time you went home.' The girl nodded, gripping his fingers tightly as he led her down to the kitchen, where Miss Lofthouse was pouring boiling water into the teapot. The old woman had wiped her face; she looked her usual self, slightly distant, as if her thoughts were elsewhere, but quite sane.

'Miss Lofthouse,' Deepbriar said. 'Would you do me a favour?'

'Of course,' she said. 'How can I help you?'

'Well, I'm taking Deirdre home, and I need to have a word with her father while I'm

238

there. I wondered if you would pop along to the police station. Constable Giddens should be there. You know him, don't you.'

'Of course I do,' she said scornfully. 'Such a pleasant young man. He's the one who took over your uniform when you bought yourself a suit.'

Deepbriar swallowed this bizarre idea without comment. 'So you won't mind going to the police station and telling him that you found Deirdre hiding in your house, and that you've sent her home.'

She tipped her head on one side and thought about it for a moment. 'I think I can do that. What about the tea?'

'Keep it hot, and you and I will share it in a few minutes.' He led the way to the back door. 'Come on, Deirdre, we'll go through the garden, and in at your side gate, so nobody will see.'

'That's right, give your mummy and daddy a surprise. Everybody loves a surprise,' Miss Lofthouse said, nodding vigorously. She put a knitted tea cosy over the pot and led the way outside, waving at Deirdre and Deepbriar before she went round to the front gate.

Deepbriar watched Deirdre run through the Grigsdykes' back door, following a moment later to find Peg, joyous tears flowing down her face, clutching her daughter to her ample chest.

'Where've you been?' Alf asked, caressing his daughter's tangled hair.

'Deirdre might talk to you about that later,' Deepbriar said, 'but right now I'd like a word with you, Grigsdyke.' He jerked his thumb at the man, summoning him outside.

'It was your fault, Alf,' Deepbriar said, when they had reached the comparative privacy of the shed at the end of the garden.

'What?' Alf's face flushed red. 'You–'

'Shut up and listen. By rights I ought to tell the chief superintendent why Deirdre ran away. And in case you haven't cottoned on yet, it was because she was afraid you'd come home drunk again. You scared the poor kid half to death last time, remember?'

'I've never laid a hand on her,' Alf protested.

'Makes no difference. Chief Superintendent Murray will probably throw the book at you, and serve you right. Two days we've spent on this search, when we've got serious cases needing our attention. Wasting police time is a serious offence. You should have told us that Deirdre had run off before.'

Grigsdyke seemed to deflate. He hung his head. 'I know the drink don't suit me, Constable, but I can't help it,' he said miserably. 'I don't mean no harm to my kids, or the missus. I love 'em, you know I do. It's just that sometimes they sets me off. They get on me nerves, like.'

'Only when you're drunk. You threatened your wife and children with a knife,' Deepbriar persisted. 'You could have killed somebody.'

'I wouldn't hurt 'em,' Alf protested. 'Never!'

'You can't be sure, not when you've had a skinful. Don't forget I know you, Alf, I've not forgotten that black eye you gave me. As for Deirdre, she was so scared, I'm not sure she wanted to come back. She's terrified of you, Alf, scared out of her wits by her own father. Aren't you ashamed?'

'All right, so I'm ruddy ashamed!' Alf roared. 'But what can I do?'

'Stop drinking!' Deepbriar shouted back. 'Sign the pledge. Swear by every last thing you can think of that you'll never come home drunk again.'

'But I'd have to give up me darts.' The man was whining now. 'It's the only ruddy thing I'm good at. When I win the rest of the team make a fuss of me. They like buying me a pint or two. There's no harm in that.'

'Oh yes, there is, for someone who can't hold his drink. Tell the team you're giving up the booze. Who's your captain these days?'

'Joe Harker. Why? Don't have me thrown out...' He looked terrified.

'I'll do worse than that. If I hear you've come home the worse for wear, just one more time, Alf, then you won't be the only

241

one who suffers. Tonight I'll be calling on Joe. I'll tell him that if he doesn't keep you sober then the team is finished, because I'll get them banned from every single pub in the county, starting with the Goose.'

'You wouldn't. You couldn't.' Alf was aghast.

'You just watch me.' Taking the man's lapels in his bunched fists, Deepbriar delivered his masterstroke. He put all the menace he could muster into his next words, thinking the stage had lost a great talent when he decided on a career in the police force. 'One more thing. If I hear so much as a whisper that you've been drinking, I'll be coming to get you. Not as a copper, but as a father; I've a little girl of my own now. A daughter's a precious thing, and if you ever frighten Deirdre again, by coming home the worse for the booze, you'll have me to answer to. You won't know what hit you, Alf.'

Feeling that he had done all he could, and, with a certain self-satisfied glow, Deepbriar left the shed and returned to Bridge House, where he quickly downed a welcome cup of tea before heading back to the police station.

'Deepbriar!' Chief Superintendent Murray's voice echoed through the police house as the constable went in through the front door. Where the blazes have you been, man? The missing child's turned up. I've had to send Giddens to see if he can catch Chief

Inspector Stubbs before he gets back to Falbrough, since it's his case. So I'm stuck here, and there's nobody to go out and tell the men at the old airfield to call off the search. No good asking you, since you can't drive.'

'I'm sorry, sir. There hasn't been much time to spare for lessons, but I could go on my bike,' Deepbriar offered.

Murray harrumphed, glowering at him. 'I suppose that will have to do. It doesn't take an intelligent man long to master a simple thing like driving a car. I've even known some women make fair drivers after a few months of hard work. You'd better pull your socks up, Constable. Driving's an essential skill these days. Go on then, call off the hunt. I suppose it's lucky you took so long over your bacon and eggs, or you'd have been out there already with the rest of them.'

More than forty-eight hours had passed since Deirdre Grigsdyke had returned home, but they were no nearer to finding the man who murdered Janey Smithers. Chief Inspector Stubbs looked at the men standing before him, waiting for total silence before he spoke. He met Deepbriar's eyes and grimaced; the constable guessed what he was about to say. Chief Superintendent Murray had just left, after a brief visit, and as the last of the light leached from the sky outside, marking the passing of another fruitless day, Stubbs made his announcement.

'We're on our own with this case from now on,' Stubbs said. 'Since the body was found on our patch there'll be no more help from Cawster unless there's some new evidence. We'll keep following up any likely cars, where we can, but other than that, we've hit a brick wall. I shall remain in command on the case for the time being, assisted by Sergeant Jakes, and Constables Tidyman and Deepbriar. The rest of you will return to normal duties, although that doesn't mean you can't keep your eyes and ears open. Anything, a whisper, the merest hint, no matter what the source, needs to be passed on.'

Deepbriar looked around at his colleagues as the chief inspector dismissed those men who would no longer be involved in the case. Every one of them knew what this meant. Officially the case was about to be written off; there was no longer much hope of finding Janey's killer.

'Right. Back to business,' Stubbs said, waving the remaining three officers into chairs around his desk. 'Sergeant, I gather you might have a bit of good news for us.'

'I hope so, sir,' Jakes said. 'I've got an address for Annie Craggs, thanks to one of her old school friends. I thought we might ask somebody from the Met to call on her.'

'No, I'd rather you went. Catch the first train in the morning. It's not as if we've any other leads. Deepbriar, while the sergeant is in London, you can call on Eddie Craggs again. See if there's anything else you can squeeze out of him.'

'Yes, sir.' Deepbriar nodded, his mind already busily working out which buses he would need to catch.

'Tidyman and I will be concentrating on the car, we still have a few tenuous leads to follow up.' Stubbs rose, and the other three men immediately got to their feet. 'We'll make an early start in the morning. I didn't say anything specific earlier, but we've been given just four more days. No new evidence by the end of that time, and the case will be put on the back burner.'

Deepbriar wheeled his bicycle out of the yard behind the police station, his thoughts far away. Beneath the streetlamp he put a foot on the pedal to mount, ready to kick off into motion, but a young woman came hurrying towards him. 'Constable Deepbriar?'

It was June Day. She had looked pretty in school uniform, but dressed in a smart coat and with her hair framing her face beneath a stylish little hat, she was positively beautiful.

'Miss Day. What can I do for you?'

'I did what you said,' the girl replied. 'I told my parents what happened. They were good about it, really. Now I want to go and see Eddie.'

'You'll need to get permission,' Deepbriar said. 'I can tell you how it's done, but you'll need your parents' approval, because of your age.'

The girl nodded. 'I guessed that.' She smiled. 'I'm working round to it, but it might take a week or two. That's why I wanted to see you, because there's something I want Eddie to know, and I thought you might tell him. I have an uncle who owns a garage. He has three or four men working for him, and he's prepared to give Eddie a job when he comes out of prison, if he promises to behave himself.'

'Eddie knows about cars, does he?'

'Yes.' She gave a little laugh. 'He tried to teach me how a motor worked once, but I didn't understand a word. He's not stupid, you know, though I don't think he learnt much about anything at school. Years ago, he used to hang around at the race track and do odd jobs for the mechanics, before one of his friends stole some tools and they were forbidden to go again.' She pulled a face. 'Annie told me Eddie wasn't involved, and I believe her; he was quite upset about it all. I think he ought to get a second chance.'

'Finding him a job just might work,' Deepbriar conceded with a smile. 'I'm not sure that young man deserves you.'

'Maybe he's worth more than you think,'

the girl replied stoutly. 'The thing is, with Eddie being on my mind so much, I remembered something that he said. One night when we were coming out of the pictures, we saw his father on the other side of the road, and Eddie started laughing. When I asked why, he said it was because he'd just been reminded of that day when he played the hero and came to my rescue. He said his dad was still wearing the hat.'

'What hat?' Deepbriar stared at her.

'The one that horrible man was wearing. Eddie knocked it into the long grass, and the man went off without it. It wasn't the sort of thing Eddie would wear but he picked it up and took it home. He gave it to his dad.'

'And when you both saw him...?'

'...Mr Craggs still had it.' June nodded. 'Do you think that might be helpful?'

Chapter Sixteen

'I'm not asking for much, Eddie,' Deepbriar said. 'A nod of the head will do. I heard that you picked up this man's hat after the tussle you had with him. Is that right?'

The young man slouching in the wooden chair remained silent and sullen. He'd barely even looked at the constable when he came in, and so far he'd not spoken a single word.

'Somebody ought to tell June Day she's wasting her time,' Deepbriar said, his irritation getting the better of him. 'The ones who say you're past saving have got it right, haven't they?'

'What do you mean? What's June got to do with anything?' Eddie glared at Deepbriar across the table, his fists bunching.

Pleased to find that he had caught the young man's attention, Deepbriar met the hostile eyes. 'She thinks you can change,' he said, keeping his tone neutral. 'She told me that when you get out of here, she'll do her best to help you go straight.'

'When did she say that?' Eddie bit savagely at a fingernail that was already down to the quick. He leant forward. 'Tell me. Please,' he added, after a moment's silence, as if the word had been dragged from him by force. 'Have you seen her?'

'She came to see me,' the constable said. 'If you want to know more, then first you answer my questions. Give and take, that's the way it works.'

There was a pause before Eddie gave a tiny nod, his eyes wary.

'Right,' Deepbriar said. 'The hat. You picked it up after the fight.'

'Yeah. I thought it might be worth something, but when I took it home my dad pinched it, so I never found out.' A bitter half-smile fleeted across his face. 'When he gets his claws into something he don't let go.'

'He still has it, then?' Deepbriar's pulse quickened. It was what June had suggested, but he'd hardly dared to hope it was true. This could be their first concrete piece of evidence.

'He did before I came in here, I've not seen him since.' He grimaced. 'Ma comes, but not the old man. Don't fancy your chances of getting that hat off him, if that's what you're after.'

'I reckon I'll find a way,' Deepbriar replied. He had the information he'd come for, but he must be thorough this time; he should have found out about the hat on his previous visit. 'Is there anything else that might help us, Eddie? What about the car? Are you sure you didn't see the registration plate? Even a couple of letters or numbers could be useful. Maybe some part of it stuck in your memory.'

Craggs shook his head. 'No.' He was quiet for a moment, his eyes focused on something far away. 'I reckon I'd know him if I saw him again.'

'First we have to find him. It's details that count, Eddie. Anything.'

'His gloves were posh,' Eddie said suddenly. 'Black leather, really thin and sort of soft, I'd never seen anything like them before.'

'What about his feet? Was he wearing boots or shoes?' Deepbriar persisted. 'And how about his trousers? Were they the same colour as the cap you saw in the car?'

Young Craggs glowered at him. 'I can't remember. I've tried, OK? There's nothing else.'

Deepbriar gave him a long steady look, and decided this was probably the truth. He sighed and put his notebook away. 'Fair enough.' Briefly, he told Eddie of the exchange he'd had with June Day the previous afternoon.

'She really said that? About getting me a job at a garage?' Eddie looked a different man, the sullenness replaced by a wistful expression that softened his sharp features.

'Every word,' Deepbriar replied, rising to his feet. 'A man would have to be a blooming fool to throw away his chances with a girl like June, but you shouldn't need me to tell you that.'

'If you see her...' Eddie began.

Deepbriar shook his head. 'Keep your nose clean and don't lose your privileges, and I reckon you'll be seeing her yourself. She's trying to get permission for a visit, and she's a determined young lady. One more thing. Where am I likely to find your father?'

The pubs had closed after lunch when Deepbriar reached Cawster, so bearing in mind what Eddie had told him about his father's habits, he decided to begin his search at the Craggs's house.

Ma Craggs opened the door with a broom in her hand. When Deepbriar asked to speak to her husband she responded with a mouthful of abuse, lifting her chosen weapon as if to bar his way.

'I only want to talk to Mr Craggs,' Deepbriar said, as the woman paused to take a breath; he was sure the man was inside. He was cross with himself; it had been a mistake to come here. It would have been far wiser to tell Chief Inspector Stubbs about the hat, so that they could go through the proper channels and get a search warrant. People like the Craggs clan were bound to be wary of the police, and they were good at making themselves scarce. As Deepbriar hesitated on the doorstep, a voice rang out from near by.

'If you're lookin' for Craggs, 'e done a bunk through the back when he saw you comin'.'

Looking round, Deepbriar located the source of this information; a woman was shaking a duster from an upstairs window on the opposite side of the street. 'About time that shifty beggar got what's coming to him. It's men like him what gives Carrside a bad name.' She pointed towards the end of the road. 'That way. Hurry up and you'll get him.'

'You interfering old hag,' Ma screamed. 'Shut your effing mouth! Think you're so special, jus' 'cos your ol' man works for the gas. Fine one to talk you are. We all know about them meters.'

Leaving the two women to their dispute, Deepbriar ran, reaching the end of the road just as Craggs climbed over his neighbour's fence. The fugitive had a head start of some fifty yards, and when he took to his heels, Deepbriar had a nasty feeling the man was going to get away from him. 'Craggs,' he bellowed as he picked up speed. 'I want to talk to you.'

Fortune was on the side of the law for once. At the far end of Cobb Road, a beat officer appeared, right in Craggs's path. The man stopped, looking to left and right, as if hoping to find an escape route. As Deepbriar closed the gap between them, he saw the indecision in his quarry's eyes; by repute, this was a man who would always choose fighting over talking, but the uniformed constable was approaching fast, and he wouldn't fancy his chances at odds of two to one, not against the law.

'I only want a word, Craggs,' Deepbriar called. 'No point making this difficult for yourself. I don't want to have to drag you down to the station when we can have a quiet chat right here.'

Craggs waited, his expression truculent.

'Causing trouble again, Craggs?' the beat officer asked, giving Deepbriar a nod of recognition. 'Anything else I can do for Falbrough CID?'

'I wouldn't mind a witness,' Deepbriar replied. 'I believe this man is in possession of crucial evidence regarding a case of murder.'

'You what?' Craggs bunched his fists and looked wildly from Deepbriar to the uniformed man and back again. It looked as if he regretted not making a fight of it. 'You're not pinnin' no murder on me!'

'Shut up and listen,' Deepbriar bellowed, cutting the man's protest short. 'That hat you're wearing. Would that be the one you took from your son seven years ago?'

Looking baffled, Craggs nodded.

With the hat in his hands a few minutes later, Deepbriar couldn't help smiling. While the amused uniformed officer looked on, Craggs had surrendered his headgear and accepted the receipt Deepbriar wrote out for him. 'And you'll come down to the station tomorrow morning,' Deepbriar said, 'so we can take a statement about how this particular item came into your possession.'

'I never knew he'd nicked it off no bloody murderer,' Craggs growled.

'Of course you didn't,' Deepbriar replied smoothly. 'Just do what you're told and there shouldn't be any need for us to charge you with receiving, not this time.'

As he rode on the bus to Falbrough, Deepbriar took the opportunity to have a proper look at his prize. The outside of the hat was so filthy that it was impossible to guess its original colour although, as June had suggested, it was dark. Turning the hat over, screwing up his nose in distaste at the grease that ringed the lining, Deepbriar prised up the inside band. Craggs had used a folded page of newspaper to make the hat fit, and this was stuck firmly to the fabric. With great care Deepbriar peeled it away. He stared in wonder at what he had un-covered, hardly able to believe his eyes. There, hidden where none would ever see it, alongside the name of an illustrious London company of hatters, was a single word, em-broidered in tiny italics, as fresh and read-able as the day the hat was sold.

'Hingham?' Chief Inspector Stubbs's brows furrowed. 'That name rings a bell.'

'Sir John Hingham was mentioned by Colonel Brightman,' Deepbriar said. 'He owns a Daimler, and he comes north for the shooting most years.'

'That's right,' Constable Tidyman said, fetching out a piece of paper from amongst the scattered piles on his desk. 'We checked. Styre Hall, Northamptonshire. The local police made enquiries as requested. Sir John's chauffeur doesn't fit the description we gave them. He's over sixty, five foot four, weighs in at about nine stone, and has been with Sir John for forty years. There's no chance that he's our man.'

'But then,' Stubbs said, 'this is a gentleman's hat, not a chauffeur's cap.' He wrinkled his nose. 'At least, it was.'

'Which suggests we might not be looking for a chauffeur at all. The killer could be a member of the family,' Deepbriar said quietly.

'It's circumstantial evidence at best,' Stubbs said. 'That hat could have been lost or given away, maybe even stolen.'

'Yes, but Sir John has a son, and I gather he has been known to drive the Daimler.' He didn't add that Jack Hingham had been Charles Brightman's comrade in arms, and his friend. The knowledge made him distinctly uncomfortable. 'I could telephone

Minecliff Manor, and see if I can get a description.'

'All right, Thorny.' Stubbs nodded. 'But please be discreet. We need to tread carefully. If this is all a coincidence then we could find ourselves in trouble. As I said, there are half a dozen ways in which that hat could have come into the possession of a total stranger, who has nothing to do with the Hingham family.'

Sergeant Jakes shook his head. 'Pretty big coincidence, sir. Man called Hingham owns a Daimler, the same as the one used to abduct Janey, and a hat with that same name inside it turns up at the scene when two girls were attacked.'

Deepbriar placed the call, putting his question to Charles Brightman. 'Right, thank you,' he said, after listening to his friend's reply. 'One more thing. Are there any other sons? Or maybe a male cousin who might join Sir John for the shooting?' He put a hand over the mouthpiece. 'Jack Hingham was in Major Brightman's regiment during the war. He's slight and fair, and six foot tall; definitely not our man. Major Brightman doesn't know the rest of the family, but he's asking the colonel.'

All eyes were on Deepbriar as he returned his attention to the telephone, and jotted down a few words. 'I see. Thank you, Charles.' He returned the receiver to its cradle. 'Sir John has another son, Frederick. Unlike Jack, he's fond of blood sports. He's a crack shot, and travels up to Beckley with his father most years. The colonel wasn't too clear about his appearance, although he doesn't think he's particularly tall, and he has dark hair.'

Styres Hall lay in beautiful rolling country, and Deepbriar's eyes widened as Chief Inspector Stubbs steered the car around the final curve in the long drive and brought it to rest on a wide circle of gravel. 'That's quite a place,' he said, looking up at the magnificent stone frontage of the house.

'Don't gawp, Constable,' Stubbs said humorously. 'We have to treat these people with the proper respect, but they're only human. Anyway, I don't want them to think I've brought the village idiot with me.'

'Sorry, sir. I promise not to tug at my forelock too often,' Deepbriar replied solemnly.

They were shown into Sir John Hingham's study, a fine room overlooking a magnificent lawn and the spread of parkland beyond. 'Chief Inspector Stubbs, you said?' The baronet was quite short and powerfully built, and he had noticeably protruding ears. Apart from the many lines drawn on his face by the years, and the fact that his hair was white, he fitted Eddie Craggs's description of June's attacker.

'I hadn't expected to see the police here again,' Sir John said, coming forward to shake Stubbs by the hand. 'Is this something else to do with our car?'

'In a way, sir, yes. I understand your chauffeur was interviewed a few days ago, but I need to know who else drives the Daimler. Your sons, perhaps?'

'Both my sons drive, but they have cars of their own.'

'That wasn't quite what I asked, sir. I need to know if either of them has driven the Daimler in the past,' Stubbs said.

'Yes, I seem to recall them driving it once or twice. Can you tell me where these questions are leading, Chief Inspector?' Some change of expression was detectable on the baronet's face. Watching him, Deepbriar suspected it was fear.

'I'm not at liberty to disclose that at the moment, I'm afraid.' Stubbs kept his tone neutral. 'I wonder if I might have a word with your elder son?'

'I'm sorry, I'm afraid Frederick isn't here. He's visiting friends in France.'

'That's a shame,' Stubbs said, his gaze wandering around the room. 'You don't have any family photographs or portraits on display, Sir John?'

'Not in this room, no. There are some in the morning room.'

'Perhaps you'd be kind enough to show

258

me a picture of Mr Frederick Hingham. Does he favour you in appearance?'

'Really, Inspector, I find your questions rather impertinent.' Sir John's mouth had thinned, and the surrounding lines seemed to be etched even more deeply into his fleshy countenance. 'I have told you my son isn't here. If you want to see him I suggest you come back in a month. I expect him to return home in time for Christmas.'

'I'm afraid our enquiries won't wait that long. I should like your cooperation, but if necessary I can request a search warrant and find a photograph that way.'

This time the change of expression was even easier to read; Sir John was angry, but he was also very worried. Without a word he left the room, returning a moment later with a photograph in a gilt frame. He handed this to Stubbs before retreating to the window, where he appeared to be studying the view, his back to the two officers.

Chief Inspector Stubbs looked at the photograph carefully before holding it out for Deepbriar to see. There was the solid figure, the black hair slicked down flat over a pale face, the slightly protruding ears, exactly as Craggs had described them.

Chapter Seventeen

'Thank you Sir John,' Stubbs said, putting the photograph down. 'Just one more thing. I'll need the address of your son's friends in France.'

'I don't know the address, I'm sorry.'

'That's unfortunate.' Stubbs voice was excessively dry. 'Exactly when did he leave, sir? Was he travelling by train?'

'He left yesterday. I believe he intended to fly.' The man's voice was cold and distant, as if he spoke with great reluctance. 'A friend of his, a man called Oliver, has an aeroplane which he pilots himself. He keeps it at an airfield somewhere to the south of here. That's all I know.'

'Then we shan't trouble you any further. Good day, Sir John.' Stubbs turned on his heel and Deepbriar followed him from the room. The butler was hovering in the hall, and came swiftly to open the door.

'Is Sir John's younger son at home?' Stubbs asked, pausing in the doorway. His tone made it clear that he would brook no evasion and, although the butler looked as if he had just swallowed a lemon, he answered quickly enough.

'Yes, sir. You'll find him in the garage.' He indicated a path along the terrace. 'Turn left at the end, past the walled garden.'

'You think our man's made a run for it, don't you, sir?' Deepbriar said quietly, as they skirted the house and came into a large courtyard.

'Possibly,' Stubbs said. 'His father suspects something; he was obviously holding back. Assuming Frederick Hingham has a guilty conscience, a visit from the local police asking about the car might have been enough to scare him into leaving the country in a hurry. Trouble is, we don't know if what Sir John told us is true. His son and heir is just as likely to be on a boat heading for the South China Seas, or on the London train, for all we know. We need to hear what the younger son has to say. If there's no love lost between the brothers, he might be more cooperative than his father.'

A tall man with pale blond hair appeared as the two officers approached the open doors of the garage. 'Jack Hingham,' he said. 'You'll excuse me if I don't shake.' He held his hands out to show that they were covered in grease. 'I enjoy tinkering.'

'That's all right, sir, we'll forgo the formalities. I'm Chief Inspector Stubbs, Falbrough CID.' He nodded at his companion. 'This is Constable Deepbriar.'

'Deepbriar! You're Charlie's friend.' The

261

man grinned. 'I've heard a lot about you. I'm really sorry I can't shake your hand. It seems strange we've never met. I was disappointed about missing Charlie's wedding, but my wife wasn't too well, and with three children it wasn't fair to leave her to cope alone.'

'You don't live here at the Hall, sir?' Stubbs asked.

'No, we have a cottage in the grounds, about half a mile away. My father was never much good with children, and mine can be rather boisterous. Besides, we prefer to be independent, insofar as we can.' He glanced at the rear of the house and his smile died. 'You're here to ask more questions about the car. When that local bobby came, I knew there were things he wasn't telling us. What's been going on?'

'We wanted to speak to your brother, but I gather he's away from home.'

'What has Frederick done?' The question was asked quietly, but with great intensity.

Stubbs hesitated. 'We are simply making enquiries,' he said.

'Please,' Jack Hingham urged, 'I need to know. Poor old Davis was quite upset when the local police came asking about the car. He drives as if he's following a funeral procession; there's no way he'd get into any sort of trouble behind the wheel. I wondered then if it was Fred who'd been up to something, it wouldn't be the first time he's been reckless on the road.' He gave a humourless smile. 'But you wouldn't have come all this way if he'd committed a traffic offence, or caused an accident. That would have been dealt with locally, which means this is something more serious.'

When the chief inspector still didn't answer, Hingham led the way to the other side of the garage and turned on a light. 'Here's the car. I had a good look round it after the police left last time, there's no sign that it's been involved in a smash, not even a dent in the bumper.'

The car gleamed, the light reflecting off highly polished black paintwork. Chief Inspector Stubbs opened the door and looked inside. 'Spotless,' he said.

'Davis doesn't have a great deal to do.' The man swallowed hard. 'Look, I wish you'd tell me something about all this.' He hesitated. 'My brother was in serious trouble once before, but the law was never involved. Maybe it should have been.'

'Why don't you tell us about it?' Stubbs prompted.

Hingham was silent a moment, then he let out a long, sighing breath. 'I suppose there's no alternative. My brother has always been a bully, Chief Inspector. I suffered at his hands many times when I was a child. Of course, that's common enough, but there were occa-

sions when he went too far. When he was
fifteen Frederick was discovered in one of
the barns with a young girl, the daughter of
a tenant farmer. He'd forced her to take all
her clothes off. It sounds innocent enough in
some lights; the girl wasn't hurt, although
that may have been because he was interrupted. He persuaded my father that it was
no more than a practical joke, and the girl's
parents were paid off and told to keep the
matter quiet.'

Turning a little away from them, he went
on, 'The girl was only ten. Frederick had
told her he'd have the whole family thrown
out of their home if she didn't do what he
wanted.' Hingham kept his gaze on the car
while he spoke. 'I'm pretty sure that wasn't
the only occasion when he tried that sort of
thing, only he became more careful. If this is
something to do with a young woman...' he
broke off and spun round to meet Stubbs's
eyes. 'Oh God.'

Deepbriar thought for a moment that the
man was going to pass out. Every vestige of
colour had drained from his face, and he
swayed where he stood. 'That little girl, the
one who was murdered. She was found near
Falbrough, wasn't she? And it happened
while Frederick and my father were shooting at Beckley.'

'You're jumping to some hasty conclusions, sir,' Chief Inspector Stubbs said.

'Right now, I'm simply asking to speak to your brother.'

Jack Hingham recovered himself a little, and his mouth twisted in what would have been a smile if it hadn't been for the bleak look in his eyes. 'I know more about my brother than you do, Chief Inspector, and I'm not a fool. Davis may be getting on a bit but he's an intelligent man and he has a good memory. Between us we worked out the significance of the dates he was asked about; they corresponded to three shoots at Beckley, when Frederick accompanied my father. The murder of that child has been all over the newspapers. Don't try to tell me this has no connection with the enquiry into her death.'

Stubbs shook his head. 'I'm afraid I can't reveal anything at this juncture, sir. If you wish to help us, then please give us any information you can about your brother's current whereabouts. I gather he's gone to France.'

'He won't be there yet.' Hingham looked at his watch. 'I doubt if he's even taken off. I've never known Olly get out of bed much before midday, even in a crisis.'

'And where exactly is the airfield?' Stubbs asked. 'Your father was rather vague about its location.'

The other man gave a humourless bark of laughter. 'That's so like my father, trying to

265

avoid telling you a direct lie. He knows where it is. Frederick has been going there a lot over the last few months. Olly has been teaching him to fly.'

'Then perhaps you'd give us directions,' Stubbs said, rather shortly.

'It's about eight miles from here, but it's difficult to find. I can show you the way if you like.' As Stubbs hesitated Hingham hurried on. 'You'll probably miss it otherwise; it's in the middle of nowhere. I've an errand to run, over in that direction. If you follow my car to the airfield I can go on from there; it's not far out of my way.'

'Very well, sir, thank you. Since we're all going to the same place, I'm sure you won't object if Constable Deepbriar travels in your car?'

Higham nodded. 'Just give me a minute to wash my hands and fetch my jacket.'

'You think he'll try to get in our way, sir?' Deepbriar asked, once the man had hurried into the back of the house.

'He definitely has something in mind. That's why you're going with him.'

Jack Hingham drove fast, but with considerably more skill than Sergeant Jakes, and after a few minutes Deepbriar found himself relaxing. 'It's beautiful country, sir,' he said, as the road wound its way across the side of a hill, giving them a wide view of the valley below.

'Yes. Though your part of the world is just as lovely in its own way; I've only been to Minecliff once, but I'd like to see more of the area. Charlie is always inviting us to visit for a few days, but it's not easy with a young family.'

'I'm sure you'd all be very welcome, sir,' Deepbriar replied. 'Mrs Brightman loves children, and when we were young the colonel never seemed to mind when there were half a dozen boys racketing around the manor.'

'Not much like my happy home then,' Jack Hingham said shortly. 'Look, Constable, I know you were sent along to keep an eye on me, and you're probably not supposed to talk to me, but I'd be very much obliged if you'd tell me the truth.'

'I'm afraid I can't do that, sir. The chief inspector would throw the book at me.'

'Drop the sir, please. If you can call Sunny Boy by his first name, then surely you can call me Jack.'

'Sonny Boy?' Deepbriar was puzzled, unable to see the connection with Charles Brightman. 'Like the song?'

'No, S-U-N-N-Y.' He glanced at Deepbriar, a half-smile on his face. 'Because of his surname. Corny, but everybody got christened with a nickname when they joined our unit, and that was the best we could come up with. So, it's Jack, right?'

'All right,' Deepbriar said reluctantly. 'And I'm Thorny, but only when the Chief Inspector's out of earshot. So, although Charlie Brightman calls you Jack, presumably he knows you as something else.'

Hingham gave a brief laugh. 'I can see what he meant about you, you're a bit sharp. OK, I'll come clean. In the mess I was called Girly. Girly Gingham, you see. But it's one of the things I was happy to leave behind me.'

'I'm not surprised,' Deepbriar said, grinning. He liked this man, and he could see how he and Charles Brightman had become friends. 'Consider it forgotten. Even after a revelation like that, though, I still can't disclose any details about our enquiry. I'm sorry.'

'Fair enough,' Hingham said. After a short pause he went on. 'There was always something about Frederick, even from his childhood – I don't know how to put it. It wasn't just that we didn't get on, there was something more than that. You'll think I'm prejudiced; younger brothers can expect to take a few knocks, but the incident with the little girl wasn't the only nasty thing he got up to.'

Deepbriar looked across at him; the other man's expression was bleak, and he was staring glumly ahead as if he wasn't really seeing the road.

'It might help if you tell me more,' Deep-

268

briar prompted.

Jack Hingham shifted in his seat and seemed to come back to himself. 'I don't see why not. When he was ten Frederick shot our father's favourite dog, and threw its body down the disused well behind the dower house. I saw him do it, but I never dared tell anybody.' He grimaced. 'Stupid, I suppose, but I was afraid he'd throw me down to join poor old Rollo if I ratted on him.'

'Why did he kill the dog?' Deepbriar asked. 'I assume it wasn't an accident?'

'No. He thought Rollo got more affection from our father than he did.' He gave an odd little laugh. 'He was probably right. For my part, I was quite happy being ignored, there are some advantages in being the younger son: less was expected of me. Not that I think Frederick's character had anything to do with our father's demands on him; they got on well enough. I was the one who was considered lacking.'

Deepbriar gazed out at the snow-covered tops of the surrounding hills. He knew he shouldn't take the risk, but every instinct told him that Jack Hingham could be trusted, and it might be useful to have this man on their side. He bit thoughtfully at his lip, then took the plunge. 'Listen, Jack. I've not been a detective long, and I'm not too familiar with the rules, but I think I'm stepping a long way over the line. What I'm about to tell you goes no further, right?'

Hingham took his eyes off the road long enough to meet his eyes. 'I really appreciate you trusting me, and I swear I'll keep my mouth shut, Thorny. I've never let a friend down. Charlie can tell you that.'

'I'll take your word for it.' Deepbriar paused, working out how much he should say. 'I'll tell you why we're interested in the dates Davis was asked about. The little girl who was murdered is known to have been taken away by car, and it was identified as being similar to the one owned by your family. Six years ago there was a very similar case.' He glanced at Hingham; the man had gone very pale. 'Maybe I've said enough?'

'No, go on,' Hingham said tautly.

'The child was abducted from pretty much the same part of town, and although no car was seen, the victim must have been taken in a vehicle of some kind, because she was spirited away very quickly. The year before that, two girls were accosted in a park. On that occasion they got lucky; the brother of one of the girls came to the rescue and gave their attacker a beating. For various reasons the incident was never investigated. It's only recently that we've been given a description of the man who was involved. And, more to the point, the car he drove was seen. There was what looked like a chauffeur's cap lying on the front seat.' He broke off there; he had already said far too much. If Chief Inspector Stubbs ever found out what he'd done, his career in CID would probably be at an end; he couldn't reveal their last and most damning piece of evidence, the scruffy old hat he had reclaimed from Eddie Craggs's father.

Jack Hingham stared bleakly through the windscreen. 'The first incident, seven years ago; that fits. It was soon after I got married, and my wife and I were staying in the hall for a few days, because there was work being done in our house. Frederick came home with a black eye and a split lip. He made up a story about a fight with two men outside a public house, making out that he'd acted the hero. I always thought it was unlikely; he claimed he'd stepped in because they were shouting obscenities at a young woman, but my brother has never had much respect for the fairer sex. In fact I'd say he's never cared much about anyone but himself.'

'One thing did occur to me, Jack,' Deepbriar said. 'If your brother was with a shooting party, how would he leave without anyone noticing? Surely the chauffeur would be waiting around in case he was needed, along with the car?'

'Frederick gets bored with bringing down driven birds; he claims it's tame. Whenever he could he'd find somewhere to go rough shooting instead. As for Davis, he's been with us so long he's inclined to take a few

271

liberties. He's a keen ornithologist, and as soon as the shooting party leaves for the day, he'll hike off in the opposite direction with a packed lunch and a pair of binoculars.' He let out a gusty sigh. 'Dear Lord, I wish it wasn't true, but you're after the right man. Thank you for confiding in me, Thorny. I swear nobody will ever know.'

There was a brief silence. They were dipping down towards a flatter landscape, and Deepbriar thought he saw a windsock flying beyond a copse of trees.

'He'll hang, won't he?' Hingham's voice was cold and flat. From the way he spoke Deepbriar knew no answer was expected, and held his peace.

'You can't begin to imagine what that will do to my father.' Suddenly Hingham put his foot on the accelerator and the car leapt forward, swinging wildly round a tight bend. There was a junction immediately on their right, and, keeping the car on the road with some magic the constable couldn't comprehend, Hingham took the turn without reducing speed.

Chapter Eighteen

'What are you up to?' Deepbriar said, looking back. The junction was already out of sight, and Chief Inspector Stubbs couldn't possibly have seen them turn off.

'Breathing space,' his companion said. 'I want a chance to talk to him. I have to try.'

'And where does that leave me?' Deepbriar demanded. 'Listen, Jack. I can't let your brother leave the country. You just told me you think he's guilty. I understand how hard that will be on you and your father, but are you ready to help a possible murderer to escape, even if he is your brother? Obstructing the police is a serious offence.'

The other man didn't answer, concentrating on his driving as they sped along winding roads, each seemingly narrower than the one before, until they were bouncing down an unmade track. Taking a final sharp bend on two wheels, the car shot between tall gates of wire mesh, propped open with milk crates. They bounced on to an area of rough grass. To their left were two aircraft hangars, while directly before them was an array of tumbledown sheds. Beside one of these a small aircraft stood with its propeller turning, a faint haze of exhaust coming from the engine. A man stood on the wing, leaning down into the cockpit so that only half of his body was visible.

Jack Hingham pulled up just as a second man came out of the near shed. He was stockily built and bare-headed, but the brisk breeze had no effect on his cap of black hair as he turned to walk to the aircraft.

Deepbriar made a grab as Hingham flung open his door and leapt from the car, but he was too late. With a muttered curse the constable went after him, but seeing he couldn't prevent the confrontation, Deepbriar slowed to a walk. It would be better not to alarm their quarry, and hope that Stubbs would arrive soon.

The two brothers had come to a halt about five yards apart. Nobody would have guessed their close relationship, the younger one willowy and fair, the elder dark and bulky. There was no hint of affection on either face as they stood staring at each other.

'Still poking your nose in, Jack?' Frederick Hingham said. 'The times I gave you a thrashing for that when you were a snot-nosed kid, but you never learnt your lesson.'

'I'm here for our father's sake, not mine,' Jack replied. 'Seeing you dragged through the courts and ending on the gallows would probably kill him.'

'Who's that?' It seemed Frederick had

noticed Deepbriar for the first time. 'No, don't tell me, he's another of those bumbling policemen. Well, you're both wasting your time, you won't stop me leaving. Look on the bright side, little brother. In a few minutes I'll be on my way, and you're never going to see me again. If you're right and the old man dies of shame, you'll be taking over the hall.'

'You're not going to get away, Frederick. The police will track you down.' Jack put a hand inside his jacket. Deepbriar couldn't see what he took out, but he took a half-step closer, unaccountably concerned.

'There's an alternative,' Jack said. 'For once in your life, do the decent thing.'

Frederick Hingham laughed. 'I'm not an idiot, Jack, I came prepared.' He reached into his pocket and brought out a gun. 'Snap! You little prig, did you really think I'd kill myself, for our father's sake? You're an even bigger fool than I took you for.' He lifted the weapon and flicked off the safety catch, with the comfortable ease of long practice. 'Seeing you standing there though, pious little beggar that you are, I must say I'm tempted to rid the house of Hingham of its second son. Maybe we should make it a bit fairer? How about a duel? I think I'm safe enough. You were always a lousy shot; too bloody squeamish to go for a kill.'

'Mr Frederick Hingham,' Deepbriar said,

moving a little closer, 'I'm here to arrest you for the murder of Jane Smithers. Why don't you put the gun down and come quietly. Aren't two deaths enough?'

'Two deaths?' the man laughed again. 'You haven't been doing your homework, Mr Policeman. I make it four. But perhaps you don't talk to your flat-footed associates over the border. Oh no, hold on, I was forgetting Davis, he makes the tally up to five.'

'You've killed Davis?' Jack Hingham's head jerked up and he took a half-step backwards. 'What sort of monster are you? For God's sake, Freddie, tell me you're lying.'

'Why should I lie?' The words were tossed back with no show of emotion. 'He knew I'd been up to something. Pious old fool, he came to me, all bloody holier than thou, and told me there were enquiries being made. He'd put two and two together, and he wanted me to give myself up. I couldn't risk him going to the police. I had my plans for getting clear, but I needed a few hours start. *"Ding dong bell, Davis went to hell,"'* he sang. 'Remember Rollo, Jack? The poor old beast's been alone all these years, but now he's got some company.'

Deepbriar began to move, edging closer to the siblings. Frederick was too busy taunting his brother to notice, while Jack stood swaying, as if this last shock was too much for him to cope with. The gun he had brought with him dangled forgotten from his fingers.

'Hello, Jack.' A new voice broke in. Olly had climbed down from the aeroplane and was coming towards them, wiping his hands on a piece of cotton waste. Evidently the noise of the engine had prevented him from hearing the exchange between the brothers. 'I didn't expect to see you here. If you and your friend are hoping for a joyride, it will have to be another day.' He came to an abrupt halt as he saw the gun in Frederick's hand. 'What's going on, Freddie? Come on, I thought you were in a hurry. Stop larking about and let's go.'

'My brother has just admitted to being a cold-blooded murderer,' Jack ground out. 'If you help him escape then you'll be for the high jump too, Olly. I suggest you get out of here before the police reinforcements turn up. They aren't far behind us.'

'Is this some kind of joke?' Olly asked uncertainly.

'You could call it that,' Frederick replied. 'No need for you to worry, Olly. You can push off. I'll pilot myself, and let you know where to pick up your old crate in a day or two.'

The man hesitated, his gaze travelling swiftly from one brother to the other. 'I don't think that's a very good idea, you've only flown solo once, Freddie. Look, put the gun

277

away. There's got to be some mistake. We can talk this through and then get going, eh?'

'No mistake, and no talking, Olly,' Frederick said. 'Do yourself a favour and get out of here, while you've got the chance.'

'Best do as he says, sir,' Deepbriar said quietly. 'Leave this to the law.'

Frederick gave a humourless laugh. 'That's the ticket, Olly. Do what the nice policeman tells you. Go on, scoot.'

Still looking bewildered, the man obeyed, and a moment later his car sped from between the sheds and out through the gates.

'So where were we? Oh yes, our duel. I suppose it's no use asking our flat-footed friend here to count for us,' Frederick quipped, lifting his arm and turning slightly to one side, in the classic pistol shooter's stance. 'Come on, Jack, act like a red-blooded man for once in your life. It's no fun if you won't even defend yourself.'

'Stop this,' Deepbriar said, his voice harsh with strain. 'Don't make things worse for yourself.'

The man didn't shift his gaze. 'They can only hang me once,' he said. 'Besides, if I get rid of the two of you, I'll have all the time I need to get to France and find a boat. They'll never catch up with me.'

The growl of a motor made itself heard over the thrum of the aeroplane's idling engine. Deepbriar's heart leapt. Stubbs had

278

arrived. Frederick's attention wavered; by the sound of it, the chief inspector hadn't stopped by the gate, but was driving straight towards them across the field.

'It's over, Hingham,' Deepbriar said. 'Five minutes from now half the local police force will be here.'

He hardly expected to be believed, but Frederick Hingham's nerve broke. Turning to run, he fired the gun wildly, and Deepbriar flung himself at Jack, so that they tumbled to the ground together. By the time they untangled themselves and discovered that they were unhurt, the fugitive was climbing into the little aircraft.

Stubbs seemed to have guessed what was happening, for the Wolseley had changed course to head for the plane. Hingham had the aircraft in motion, taxiing towards the beginning of the grass runway. Deepbriar half-expected the chief inspector to come to a halt, but he drove on, the car bouncing with spine-jarring force as it hit tussocks of rough grass.

Deepbriar began to run, but trying to catch the aircraft on foot was futile. He turned to Jack Hingham, who had dropped to his knees. The gun lay forgotten beside him. 'You'd better put that thing away before the chief inspector sees it,' Deepbriar advised, but the man didn't seem to hear. He was staring into space, and there were tears running down his cheeks.

'Jack?' Deepbriar took hold of his shoulder. 'Come on.'

'He killed him.' Hingham's gaze was fixed far away, as if he wasn't aware of Deepbriar's presence. 'Davis was like a father to me, the father I never had. How could he do that?'

'I don't know, but right now we need to stop him.' Deepbriar stared across the airfield. Stubbs was still in pursuit of the plane, which was now speeding along the runway; he had no hope of winnng the race. Even if he managed to conjure up more speed, short of ramming the car into the tailplane there didn't seem to be much he could do.

'He'll have to turn round,' Jack Hingham said suddenly, getting to his feet. 'Look at the windsock. There'll be a hell of a downdraught off the hill. He can't take off that way.'

The little craft raced on, almost to the end of the runway, then abruptly became airborne, soaring towards the freedom of the sky. Some distance behind, Stubbs stopped the Wolseley and got out to watch.

'He's getting away,' Deepbriar said.

Beside him Jack shook his head. 'No. It'll hit him, any second now.' Even as the last word left his mouth the little plane lurched. Its nose was still pointing skywards, but the machine staggered again, as if punched by the hand of an invisible god, and began to fall from the sky.

The inexperienced pilot had lost control. As the plane fell one wing dipped, slicing at the ground. The little craft cart-wheeled, bits of metal flying into the air as it turned over twice before landing upside down. The sound of the crash was strangely muted, ripped away by the wind. Deepbriar thought how strange it was that he could still hear the engine, then he realized that the noise was being made by the police car. Stubbs was back behind the wheel, careering towards the wreck.

'Your car,' Deepbriar said urgently. 'Come on.'

Hingham shook his head. 'No,' he said. Turning his back on Deepbriar, he walked slowly away across the wilderness of long grass.

'Jack!' The constable made half a move to go after the man, but turned and ran towards Hingham's car instead. It was hardly the time to test his laughably poor skills behind the wheel, but the chief inspector might need his help.

Deepbriar got the car moving, and into second gear. Far across the airfield he saw Stubbs, out of the car now and running towards the wreck, where a thin plume of smoke was spiralling into the air. Sweat ran down Deepbriar's back. The plane would have a full tank of fuel, and there was a flicker of red showing among the wreckage. Concern for his superior's safety should have overcome his terror of driving, but it held him in a vicelike grip. It took a tremendous effort of will to pull his left hand off the wheel and change gear.

He was almost at the runway. The little car leapt forward; the ground seemed to be rushing beneath him in a green blur. He had to turn. Wrenching at the wheel, his hands gripping so tightly that they hurt, Deepbriar swung the car round. It tilted crazily, and in that second, that tiny interval between safety and disaster, the revelation came. Understanding struck like a bolt of lightning; he knew where his terror had come from, and in that same instant, it was cured.

By some miracle the car had remained on four wheels, just as the colonel's old Humber had done all those years before, when he and Charles had set it into motion in the paddock behind the manor. How they had started the car and put it into gear he didn't recall; probably they'd worked it out together, one operating the pedals, the other taking the gear lever. They had plunged down the slope, completely out of control, with the engine roaring and the ground flying by at an impossible speed. He must have buried the memory deep. It had been too terrifying for a child to contemplate; they had been seconds away from death, only yards from the deep waters of the lake when he had somehow changed the car's course.

Relief brought a wild laugh to Deepbriar's lips as he hurtled down the runway, travelling faster than he had ever done in his life. It seemed to take no more than a few seconds to reach the Wolseley; triumphantly he slammed his feet on the pedals. As the car stopped he flung open the door and was almost thrown out as the vehicle jolted; he'd forgotten to put it out of gear.

There were more important things to worry about. Chief Inspector Stubbs had vanished under the cloud of thick smoke that surrounded the remains of the plane, and the flames licking across the grass were almost at Deepbriar's feet.

'Sir?' he shouted. 'Where are you?' The air was hot, and it was hard to breathe.

'Give me a hand!' Relieved to hear Stubbs's call, Deepbriar dived into the murk and was brought up short when he collided with somebody. 'Careful, man,' Stubbs said. Coughs racked him. He grabbed Deepbriar's arm and pulled him to where Frederick Hingham was lying, half in and half out of the wreck, only feet from a roaring inferno. Between them the two officers pulled the man free, dragging him beyond reach of the flames. Hingham's nose was bleeding freely and was obviously broken, but otherwise he had no visible injuries.

'He must have given his face quite a knock,' Deepbriar said.

'No, that was me. Silly fool threatened me with a gun.' Stubbs swiped at one of the black scorch marks on the sleeve of his coat and scowled. 'I should have left him to fry.' He looked at the car Deepbriar had driven, glancing around before turning back to his junior officer. 'Where's the brother?'

'Back there.' Deepbriar nodded in the direction of the man who lay between them. 'He told us he killed Davis, to keep him quiet. I think that was one shock too many.'

'What were you playing at, losing me on the way here?'

'There was nothing I could do, sir, I'm sorry. Jack wanted to persuade his brother to give himself up.'

'Humph. Wasted his time, didn't he? It looked as if our villain was ready to shoot him.' Stubbs grimaced. 'Money, titles, what's it all worth, eh? Give me a simple life and a spot of brotherly love any day.'

Deepbriar nodded. Brotherly love had given them the breakthrough in this case; but for Eddie Craggs, they might still have no idea who had murdered Janey Smithers.

In a rare moment of optimism he found himself believing that June Day would stand by her young man. Even if she didn't, perhaps something could be done for Eddie.

Most men were capable of redemption, given the right circumstances. His glance fell on the man at his feet, just beginning to stir, and he shook his head. Most, but not all.

The publishers hope that this book has given you enjoyable reading. Large Print Books are especially designed to be as easy to see and hold as possible. If you wish a complete list of our books please ask at your local library or write directly to:

Magna Large Print Books
Magna House, Long Preston,
Skipton, North Yorkshire.
BD23 4ND

This Large Print Book, for people
who cannot read normal print,
is published under the auspices of

THE ULVERSCROFT FOUNDATION